"You Don't Want Me To Go.

If you're honest with yourself, you want to know what it would be like."

Yes, she had wondered, dreamed. But that didn't mean anything could or would happen.

She'd always assumed when she chose to take a lover that she would be so certain, all of her doubts would vanish. Not that she'd decided one hundred percent to take Zach as her lover, but she was inching closer and closer.

"We're so different, Zach."

He stepped closer. "Then why aren't you pushing me away?"

Between his sultry words, that crisp scent of his cologne and his potent touch, Ana only knew her body was heating and an ache she hadn't known had taken over.

"I'll go if you tell me to," he murmured a second before his lips came down onto hers.

Dear Reader,

If you read *From Boardroom to Wedding Bed?* you're already familiar with Cole's twin, Zach Marcum. If there were ever a character I wish I could make real, it would be this motorcycle ridin', tight T-shirt wearin' bad boy. He is sexy personified with his peekaboo tat and stubbled jawline. :)

Zach loves everything about his life: independence, women, his Harley, women, fast cars, money and, you guessed it, women! But when Ana disrupts his perfectly laid plan of seduction, he's caught off guard and for once in his life has no clue how to react to a woman.

I loved Anastasia Clark from the moment this feisty redhead entered my life. She's the perfect match for Zach with her quick wit and take-charge attitude. These two couldn't be more opposite in their personal lives, but dig a little deeper to their hearts and you'll see just how they complete each other.

I fell deeper and deeper in love with this couple as they started on two completely different paths until they came together in the end. There's nothing like the innocence of a woman to tame a sexy playboy!

I hope you enjoy Ana and Zach's journey as they discover that little piece of themselves they didn't know was missing.

Happy reading!

Jules

JULES BENNETT

HER INNOCENCE, HIS CONQUEST

Harlequin®

Desire

Recycling programs
for this product may
not exist in your area.

ISBN-13: 978-0-373-73094-0

HER INNOCENCE, HIS CONQUEST

Copyright © 2011 by Jules Bennett

www.eHarlequin.com

Printed in U.S.A.

Books by Jules Bennett

Desire

Seducing the Enemy's Daughter #2004
For Business...or Marriage? #2010
From Boardroom to Wedding Bed? #2046
Her Innocence, His Conquest #2081

JULES BENNETT

Jules's love of storytelling started when she would get in trouble as a child and would tell her parents her imaginary friend Mimi did it. Since then, her vivid imagination has taken her down a path she'd only dreamed of.

When Jules isn't spending time with her wonderful, supportive husband and two daughters, you will find her reading her favorite authors. Though, she calls that time "research." She loves to hear from readers! Contact her at julesbennett@falcon1.net, visit her website at www.julesbennett.com or send her a letter at P.O. Box 396, Minford, OH 45653.

To my sister, Angel, and best bud, Erin.
Thanks for the laughs, the brainstorming,
the movie nights, but most of all...CAKE!
I wouldn't make it through this without you crazy guys. :)

Huge thanks to my editor, Charles Griemsman,
for the insightful book on Miami life. I'm ready to move!

And last, big thanks to Roxanne St. Claire
for setting me straight on the seasonal weather in Miami
when she said they only have two seasons:
hot and hell. Thanks, Rocki!

One

"That's what I like to see. The foreman watching over her crew."

"Forewoman." Anastasia Clark concentrated on the swift work of her men and tried to keep her eyes off the broad-shouldered man who'd sidled right up against her. "You seem to keep making that blunder."

"So I do."

Risking a glance, Ana darted her gaze to the side. Zach Marcum was just as rugged and, dammit, sexy as he had been the last time she'd seen him in Victor Lawson's office nearly two years ago. Why did she have to find him so attractive?

"Let's step into your office," he told her, peering at her through his dark sunglasses. "We need to discuss some things."

Ana clutched her clipboard to her chest as she turned fully to face him. "We can't talk here?"

Who knew what went on behind those mirrored aviator shades he wore, but she was thankful she didn't have to look at him eye to eye. Those dark, exotic eyes could cause a woman to go utterly speechless. Any other woman, not her.

God help her. They didn't raise men this sexy where she was from in the Midwest.

Zach's mouth quirked up. "No, it's hot."

He turned on his work-booted heel and headed in the direction of her small trailer as if she were just supposed to fall in line simply because he said so. He was just like her father. Just because she found him one of the sexiest men she'd ever seen, didn't mean she thought his cocky attitude was acceptable.

Never in all of her life had she ever dealt with a project manager with such arrogance...or sex appeal. She had to omit that last thought from her mind or she'd have more to worry about on this job than Miami's daily afternoon rain.

If Victor Lawson hadn't been the world-renowned billionaire hotelier building this resort, Ana would've declined without hesitation.

She had plenty of work and more than a steady income, especially since she didn't spend on frivolous things. Every bit she made after bills—and her father's gambling counted as a bill—went into stocks, savings or to her mother.

But the meeting with Victor and The Marcum Agency forced her to face reality. This project would boost her reputation into amazing territory. Zach's twin, Cole, and his fiancée, Tamera, were the designing architects and wonderful people. And, from what Ana had heard, the couple had been reunited thanks to Victor Lawson hiring both The Marcum Agency and the architectural agency Tamera previously owned.

Ana hadn't met the Marcum twins' younger sister, Kayla, but she'd only heard amazing things about her as well.

Which left Zach. There was one in every family. One person who just had to be the star of every show, the flashy one, the one with all the attention, deserved or not.

Zach was a complete replica of her father—or at least the man her father used to be before he gambled away everything they owned. A handsome man who had more money than he knew what to do with so he flaunted everything he could, including and especially his charms, knowing the women would simply flock to his side.

Well, if Zach thought that's how she worked, he had another think coming. She was and always had been a professional. And she'd be damned if she'd let Zach and his architectural ego mess with her mind or the most important project she'd ever had the opportunity to contract.

She didn't have just herself to think of. She had a crew of men and women with families who depended on her. Not to mention her father, who had already called her seeking another ten thousand. If Ana's mother would just leave the man, Ana would pay for anything for her. All the money going to front her father's habit could be used to put her mother in the house of her dreams. And her father could fend for himself. He was long past due to stand up and act like the man he claimed to be.

Turning in her dusty boots, she followed Zach into her on-site office.

He'd already entered, making himself at home by taking a seat in an old yellow vinyl chair opposite her desk.

"What's up?" she asked, closing the door behind her to keep in the refreshing air-conditioning.

He slid those sexy sunglasses off his face, tossed them onto the drafted plans on her desk. He then had the gall to rake that heavy-lidded bedroom gaze over her face as if he expected her to get turned on and swoon.

The hellish Miami heat must be getting to her. She nearly did swoon.

"Did I do something to you?"

Stunned at his blunt question, Ana jerked back a bit. "Excuse me?"

Zach's hands rested on his narrow, denim-clad hips. "I've always been a good people reader. Comes from being the quiet one in the family, always sitting back and observing. What I'm getting from you is that you don't care much for me."

Nearly choking on her laughter, Ana propped a hip on the corner of her desk. No way was she going to sit completely down. She had to keep the upper hand here, on her turf. Instead of smacking him in the head with her clipboard, she professionally and calmly laid it on her desk.

"Zach, I hardly know you. I have no problem with you or our working relationship."

He stepped closer, his brows drawn together as if assessing her. "No, the issue isn't our working relationship. You're one of the most professional companies I've worked with, thus far. It's you. There's something about the way your back straightens, that defiant tilt of your chin when I come around. It's subtle, but your attitude is a bit forced professionally which makes me wonder what you're compensating for."

"Attitude?" she repeated. "Let's not get into attitudes or personal assessments. Is that all you came here for?"

"Where is the rest of your crew?"

Ana didn't fidget with her hands like she wanted to. No way would she let Zach know she was nervous or edgy.

"My crew will be here within the week." She looked him dead in the eye, even though it cost her heart extra beats. "We are finishing up another project in Seattle and the rain up there has put us behind by a month. Mother Nature doesn't care about deadlines."

Zach closed the gap between them, rested his hands on the edge of her desk, right next to her hip. "You are putting a multimillion-dollar deal on the line because you can't work through the weather?"

Now she rose to her full height, which still came in a good

three inches below his. "I can work through anything, Mr. Marcum, and remain within budget and deadline."

A smile broke through the ruggedness of his stubbled face. "There's that slight attitude switch again. You're getting all worked up and you called me Mr. Marcum. It was Zach just a few minutes ago."

Millionaire or not, Zach had a bad-boy side that made her want to scream. Why did he have to have so much sex appeal? And most importantly, why did he have to know it?

No, the most important point, she argued with herself, was why did she find him so damn attractive and infuriating at the same time?

"May as well call me Zach," he continued with that cocky grin. "We'll be seeing so much of each other until this project is complete that we'll practically be married."

Ana smoothed stray hairs off her sweaty forehead and gave him her sweetest, sarcastic smile. "Lucky me."

"I knew you'd come around," he mocked. "The concrete will be delivered on Monday. Your crew will be available then, I assume?"

Ana nodded, keeping her mouth shut. Even though he was professional in every aspect, his personality grated on her nerves. Even so, she couldn't let it show, but she would make him choke on his charm. She refused, *refused* to let him see just how he affected her feminine, non-businesswoman side.

She wondered if any woman ever threw what he offered back in his face. Probably not. And not that he was offering her anything by any means. God knew she was just one of the guys, always had been. She'd grown up on construction sites and always seemed to blend in.

But how easy it would be to fall for the sexy, bad-boy image he portrayed—and portrayed well—knowing all the while beneath the well-worn jeans and black fitted T-shirt a millionaire businessman lurked. Ana bet he lived up to the total bad-boy persona and rode a Harley and had at least one tattoo. Oh, what she wouldn't give to explore his body to find that ink.

"You're overheating."

She jerked her attention back to him. "What?"

His hand came up to her cheek. "You're too hot. Get some water."

Get some… What? God, she couldn't think. Not when his thumb caressed her heated skin. If he didn't stop, a little flush would be the least of her worries.

How in the world could her body betray her like that? She couldn't, wouldn't, fall in line with what she was sure was a long trail of busty bimbos tripping over each other to fall at Zach's feet.

"I'm fine," she insisted, swatting his hand away. "I need to get back out there."

"You'll get a drink of water before you fall over in this heat." He moved to the small fridge beside her desk and pulled out a bottle of water. "Drink. I can't have my forewoman out of commission before the first beam is raised."

Taking the bottle from his hands, she twisted the cap, knowing he was right. "Thanks."

The cold, refreshing water was what she needed, but no way would she admit that to Mr. Overinflated Ego. And she certainly wouldn't admit that his touch had affected her in ways the heat of the scorching Miami sun in June couldn't.

Mercy, the man was potent. And she'd thought his looks were sinful. Maybe he deserved that cocky attitude he sported.

"Better," he commented, still studying her face. "You need to keep water with you in this weather."

"I have a cooler out there for me and my crew. This isn't my first job, you know."

His breathtaking smile widened. "Yes, I know your reputation."

What in the world did that mean? The sultry tone, the way he cocked his head to the side made his words take on a whole new meaning. He acted as if he knew who she'd been intimate with. Surely he wasn't going to get personal with her...was he?

Tingles shot through her body from the top of her overheated head to the soles of her feet. She didn't want these uninvited emotions. Didn't have time for such nonsense. She worked with sexy, cocky men on a daily basis, but for some reason Zach's heavy-lidded gaze, his shadowed jaw and all that alpha attitude made her tingle in spots she didn't know could tingle.

"Mr. Marcum—"

"Zach," he interrupted.

"Zach. As much as I'd love to sit in here and sip water in front of that air conditioner, I really need to get back out there. Was there anything else you desire?"

The arrogant smile disappeared, replaced by a slight shrug of his shoulder. "My desires are endless, but we'll start with keeping you hydrated."

She'd seriously have to watch her wording around this man, but she had a terrible feeling anything around him could be a double entendre.

Ana capped the water bottle and led the way to the door. She opened it, gesturing for Zach to pass through.

"See you tomorrow," he called as he strode to his flashy motorcycle that no doubt cost more than some of her crew's yearly wages. Perhaps she should load up on the cold water. Between watching that man saunter away and the unbearable heat, she'd need all the hydration she could get.

But she quickly reminded herself that her father had all the charm in the world. He'd once been at the top of his game, too, in his own construction career. But his gambling habit and his love of numerous women shattered any hero status Ana had given him.

A psychiatrist would have so much fun in her head. But she didn't need to pay some stranger to tell her she had commitment issues because her father had shattered her world by destroying her faith. Nor did she need them to tell her she lived a simple life, even though she had money to be extravagant, because she didn't want to get pulled into a world she couldn't control.

She turned back to the site, but her body tingled all over again at the sound of the roaring engine as Zach sped away on his bike. Mercy, that man made an impact even when he wasn't in sight.

Sexual harassment. That's precisely the lawsuit he was going to get slapped with if he didn't quit antagonizing Ana. His flirtations had been subtle, especially for him, but he just couldn't separate business and pleasure when it came to Miss Anastasia Clark.

But how could he keep his distance? He was architectural project manager, after all. Granted, he was finding mundane reasons to stop by and the project was only in the second week of construction.

And if the rest of her crew didn't show by the week's end, she'd be seeing a whole lot more of him. Personal aspect aside, this project had to be flawless, within budget and on time.

Today, though, he was glad he'd stopped by on his way into the office. Damn fool woman was on the verge of heatstroke.

A distressed damsel…his favorite kind. Women like that appreciated all his assistance and in turn, fell for his charms.

Zach nearly laughed. He had a feeling Ana didn't fall as easily as most women, nor would she appreciate his help. No, from what little he'd been around her, he knew she was independent, stubborn and private. That was the type of woman from whom he should duck for cover, but he found himself wanting to dig deeper, to uncover her secrets.

She had a vulnerability about her, something that reminded him of his baby sister. Both women wanted to be so strong, call all the shots, but they still had a gentleness about them.

Ana wouldn't like that he'd zeroed in on that trait so quickly after meeting her, but he understood her kind…. He was a master of hiding feelings himself. Wasn't he still confused and intrigued by his ex-wife? A woman who slid out of his life as easily as she had slid in and had recently returned wanting him back? How pathetic was that whole situation? She may want him back, but Zach refused to put himself on the line like that again. Sometimes in life second chances were necessary, but his ex-wife would not get another chance to hold his heart. Not after she left town with a guy Zach at one time considered a friend, leaving behind only a pathetic note.

Turning to much more pleasing matters, Zach didn't miss the fact that Ana damn near combusted when he'd caressed her flushed cheek. Her moment of silence wasn't only due to her being overworked and overheated.

And that was just one more thing about her that intrigued him. He'd worked with women before, but skinny white tanks and well-worn jeans never looked so good on any of them. Maybe it was all that deep crimson hair Ana had piled in a curly mess atop her head. Maybe it was the way she silently challenged him both professionally and personally.

Yeah, he was in for it. Anastasia was definitely a what-you-see-is-what-you-get girl even though she tried to hide her private and personal life.

The flashy socialites he was used to were shallow, no digging deep there. And that was the best kind. They always knew the rules up front. He didn't do relationships, didn't do marriage. Fun times were all he wanted in his future.

But something about peeling away Ana's intriguing layers

had him smiling. The passion she no doubt buried deep would be amazing if he could just get to it. She would be another perfect distraction—and there had been plenty of distractions lately—to get his mind off his ex, Melanie.

Zach pulled into his designated parking slot at The Marcum Agency, noting Cole's empty spot. Now that his twin brother was engaged to his college sweetheart, Tamera Stevens, Zach was seeing less and less of him.

Good for them, so long as the lovebirds didn't try to play matchmaker. Every time someone found love, they assumed every single person in their life was looking, too. Quite the opposite, in fact, for Zach. He wanted to remain single. Actually he loved every minute of being a bachelor—that way he could nurse his heart privately, put it back together piece by shattered piece and never give it out again.

Zach made his way up to his office, nodding to his assistant, Becky. As usual she was on the phone making appointments, taking new client questions and scheduling meetings with contractors.

He closed the door to his office, which might not have been the smartest move considering he was now alone with his thoughts and, once again, his thoughts circled back to Miss Clark and her dark red curls. She certainly had the proverbial temper that went along with the hair, but he had a feeling calling her on that stereotypical assessment would be detrimental to their working relationship, not to mention any personal involvement he wished to have.

Ana's quick temper and attitude rivaled that of his ex-wife. Perhaps that's why his mind kept going back to Ana, and why he both had an issue with her and was attracted to her from the get-go.

Was it her fault she reminded him of the woman who'd left before the ink on their marriage license dried? No, but it was her fault that he couldn't get her off his mind. If she weren't so damned intriguing, there wouldn't be a problem.

That irked him. What irked him even more was how one person could remind him of both his sister whom he loved with his whole heart and the woman who had shattered him to pieces.

But Ana had the best reputation in the business and had never had even one complaint about her work ethic or the finished product. Ana's construction company was one of the top in the nation and he knew he'd made the right choice in accepting her bid—even though this was the biggest project she'd ever tackled, he and Cole had faith she would work that much harder. He knew she'd started her company from scratch and built it up herself, one beam at a time. He couldn't help but admire that, considering he, Cole and Kayla had built their own firm on nothing but hopes and prayers as well.

But the woman had his thoughts all jumbled together. He didn't know if he wanted to pursue her or avoid her like the plague. Oh, well, he had a year or more to figure that out. Not that he'd ever taken that much time getting to know a woman. The chemistry was either there or it wasn't. In this case, the chemistry was most definitely there.

Zach sat down at his desk, pulled up the spreadsheet on his computer and checked to see where they were on the schedule.

If Ana's crew came even a week late, they would still be ahead of schedule, but he wouldn't let up. If he slacked now, the whole project could fall behind. On time or early was the only way he would work. Especially with Victor Lawson.

The man had the capabilities to launch The Marcum Agency and Ana's company, Clark Construction, into a whole new stratum of clientele. Just another reason to remain close to Ana's side.

"Zach."

His assistant's voice cut through his thoughts. He pressed the intercom button. "Yes, Becky?"

"Miss Clark is on line one."

Did the woman have a sixth sense where he was concerned? Here he was thinking about her at the precise time she decided to call and interrupt the beginning of what was sure to have been a wonderful daydream.

"Put her through."

He picked up the receiver, pressed the button. "Anasta-sia."

"Zach, we've got trouble."

Two

He sat straight up in his chair. "What is it?"

"There's a tropical storm moving toward Miami."

"I hadn't heard about it," Zach stated, fingers moving swiftly over his keyboard to look at a weather map. "How far out is it?"

"We've got a few days before it reaches us," she explained. "There's still a chance it'll turn or break up, but I wanted your opinion. To be honest, I'm not that experienced in tropical storms seeing as how I'm originally from the Midwest."

Zach blew out a breath, not too worried once he saw the green blob on the radar map. "They are pretty common, but we certainly can't afford to lose time. The good news is we don't have any actual structure up, so if it does reach land, there should be little damage, if any."

"Hopefully this will be the worst of Mother Nature's fury and any storms will miss us when we actually start on the construction," Ana added.

He closed the screen. "We'll keep an eye on it. For now, though, continue as planned."

She hesitated and Zach wasn't sure if she'd heard him until she said, "Um…sounds good. Thanks."

The pause she gave, as well as the shaky response, intrigued him. Gone was the firm, confident Ana. Interesting, he thought. Unchartered territory unsettled the hard-as-steel forewoman.

He disconnected the call just as his brother strode into his office.

Zach smiled, leaned back in his seat and crossed his ankle over his knee. "Well, good to see you in the office."

Cole's wide grin obviously couldn't be contained. "Sorry I've left this project in your hands, but Tam needed a break after her father's passing."

Cole's wife, Tamera, had lost her father to lung cancer a month ago. Because Cole and Tamera had recently been reunited, they took a much-needed vacation to Aruba after working on the design for the Miami resort.

"I understand. How's she doing?"

On a sigh, Cole eased himself into the leather club chair across from Zach's desk. "She's holding up. I honestly think the discovery that her father was behind me breaking off our engagement eleven years ago was almost as much of a blow to her as Walter's death."

Tamera's late father had nearly altered her and Cole's future by coming between them when they were college sweethearts. But fate's gentle hand guided them back together after eleven years of separation. Walter hadn't wanted Cole to marry his daughter, hadn't wanted a man who couldn't financially provide when he was too busy caring for his siblings after his parents' death.

Zach knew the two had loved each other and the breakup nearly caused Cole to have a nervous breakdown. But the man had just worked harder as he and Zach finished college and started their own firm.

Cole had never been the same since calling off the engagement years ago, but now that he had Tamera back in his life, Zach's twin was in a much better place.

Okay, so maybe love was meant for some people. But very few.

"You're good together," Zach observed. "She's strong and you're there for her. She'll get through this."

Cole nodded and motioned toward the blueprints spread across Zach's desk. "How's everything coming at the site?"

"No glitches yet." Zach gazed down to the design. "I feel like a kid waiting on Christmas. I just can't wait to see this completed."

"We all feel that way." Cole lifted a brow. "Want to tell me what's bothering you?"

Damn. He hated this whole "twin intuition" thing they had always shared. Some people rolled their eyes or laughed at the idea that twins could actually share a bond that deep, but Cole and Zach knew it was possible.

"She shouldn't be so fascinating," Zach blurted out. "Why does she have to get under my skin? And, more importantly, why do I let her?"

Cole chuckled. "We're talking about the forewoman? Anastasia?"

Zach blew out a breath. "Yeah."

"She is attractive," Cole agreed. "But not your typical choice. What's got you so riled up all of a sudden?"

"I can't put my finger on it."

God knew he'd spent countless moments trying to pinpoint exactly what it was about Ana that made her the subject of every blasted thought lately.

"Perhaps she's immune to your charms and that's what's gotten you so bothered." Cole smirked at Zach's scowl. "Just a suggestion. Or maybe you're drawn because she's strong-willed. Like Melanie."

Cole rarely mentioned Melanie's name. And even though he wasn't far from the truth, Zach refused to respond. Silence spoke volumes, though.

"Seriously." Cole leaned forward, his elbows on his knees. "Maybe she is the one who will finally push you over that last hurdle to get over your ex-wife. I doubt Ana is like the typical giggly gold diggers you've been seeing."

True, Ana had been matching Zach instead of allowing him to keep control of their conversations. She'd been an equal. With her take-charge attitude, Ana wasn't about to let her guard slip, especially where a man was concerned.

Something about her almost seemed hard in that aspect. Had something happened in her past? Perhaps just working for so many years around manly men had put that hard edge to her personality.

Who knows? More importantly, why the hell was he spending so much time trying to dissect someone who technically worked for him? All he wanted was a little one-on-one contact.

"I won't deny she's sexy as hell," Zach told his brother. "But she's controlling and all business."

"And you have a problem with all business, don't you?"

"Only when that stiff side comes from a stunning, frustrating female I'm going to be working with for the next year." Zach stared at his brother across the desk. "I just need to consider Ana one of the guys and forget that she looks like a woman who should be wearing diamonds and dresses instead of a hard hat and a tool belt."

Cole leaned forward, his hands flat on the glass-topped desk. "Why forget about it? Why not present an opportunity for her to be that diamonds-and-dress woman? I mean, if you can't get that image out of your head, maybe there's a reason."

Zach nearly laughed at the thought. "You're in love and it's hindering your thought process. Ana would spit in my eye if I suggested I take her out."

"Sounds like you're scared of the possibility."

Zach glared. "I'm not scared of anything."

"Prove it. Take her to the party Victor is throwing next weekend. Call it business, if that makes you feel better."

Zach laughed. "Why the hell are we even talking about this? She's not my type, so it shouldn't matter what she looks like in a formal atmosphere. I'm more concerned about what she looks like in a much more intimate setting."

Cole eyed him, the smirk still in place. "We're talking about it because you can't get her off your mind. If you think you can't get her to be your date, then don't worry about it. She's probably not interested anyway. And we both know that's exactly what this all boils down to."

Not interested? That wasn't possible. He'd seen the way her pulse kicked up, her breath hitched when he'd rubbed her cheek. No, Ana was most definitely interested.

So what did he intend to do about it?

Pathetic. Utterly and completely pathetic.

Zach found himself, for the second time today, heading toward the mysterious redhead surveying the construction site as she stood between two of her crew members. Two men who towered over her and stood just a bit too close.

Okay, so jealousy wasn't pretty. He wasn't admitting to that severe emotion. But he didn't like that she considered herself "one of the guys." She was anything but.

And so what if Cole's mocking words fueled his already raging fire? He refused to believe he was here because his twin planted a seed of doubt in his head about being able to get Ana to date him. Why did he care what she thought of him?

Because for some reason she already showed disdain to-

ward him and he hadn't done a damn thing to her. Obviously she'd had a bitter experience, probably with some jackass on the job site, and now he'd stepped in, ready to charm her into spending some intimate time together for the next several months of the project. Perfect timing. Was she worth the trouble of proving himself?

Dammit. He'd never felt the need to prove himself to anyone before.

"Zach."

Breaking through his thoughts, and halting his steps toward Ana, Zach turned his attention from the sexy forewoman's sweet denim-clad backside. His sister, Kayla, stepped from her pearl-colored four-door sedan looking beautiful as always with her dark hair smoothed back from her delicate face. With her bright pink suit and shiny silver heels, she certainly didn't belong on the dusty, filthy construction site. Good thing she was more the decorator for their firm. She certainly added beauty to everything around her simply by being there.

"I just missed you at the office." Kayla closed the gap between them and smiled. Then she turned her attention over Zach's shoulder toward Ana. "Hi, we haven't formally met yet. I'm Kayla Marcum. You must be Anastasia Clark."

Zach hadn't even heard Ana approach. He turned his body so he could see both women.

"You can call me Ana."

The two women smiled at each other and Zach couldn't help but notice they were both so different, yet equally as striking and vibrant. Even though Kayla was polished to a shine and never anything less than perfect, Ana's fit body and well-toned arms proved she cared just as much about how she looked and that she was polished herself—in a whole other way. And he certainly didn't think any "sisterly" thoughts about Miss Clark.

"What did you need?" Zach asked his sister.

Off in the distance one of the men whistled, and not a

"whistle while you work" kind. This was the stereotypical wolf whistle.

Zach didn't turn to see what unprofessional jerk had made the tacky gesture, but he did notice Ana excuse herself and march over to a group of men setting up barriers and preparing the perimeter of the structure for the concrete.

"Sorry," Zach said.

Kayla shrugged. "No need for you to apologize."

"I'm apologizing for mankind in general. That's rude."

His baby sister rolled her eyes and smiled. "Like you've never whistled at a woman before?"

"Guilty, but I haven't for a long time because I realized how disrespectful it was."

Kayla peered over Zach's shoulder. "Looks like Ana has the situation under control."

Zach turned, surprised to see Ana off to the side with a young, twentysomething man, her hands on her hips, shoulders back. He couldn't hear the words, but from the look on the employee's face, he was not on the receiving end of a pleasant conversation.

Oh, what Zach wouldn't give to be able to listen in on that tongue-lashing. Women in power were nothing short of sexy, he thought, so long as he remained in control.

Zach focused his attention back on Kayla. "What did you need me for?"

"Oh, I wanted to let you know I had to go out of town for another buying trip. I'm leaving now. The jet is waiting for me."

She eyed him with those wide, rich eyes, grinned, and Zach's stomach clinched in a most uncomfortable knot. She always got that look before she asked an unfavorable favor. He didn't even want to know what put that evil sparkle in her eye, but he had a feeling he was about to find out.

"No," he said before she could even ask whatever question she had swirling around in her pretty little head.

A smile spread across her face as she cocked her head to the side. "I'll email you a detailed list of everything you need to know."

"No."

"Please?"

"No."

"Cole would do it for you," she insisted with just enough of a pout to be cute and impossible to say no to.

Zach laughed. "First of all, I'm never getting married. Second of all, Cole would never, *ever* coordinate a wedding shower."

Kayla sighed in frustration. "I didn't ask you to coordinate it. I just need you to work on a few details for me while I'm gone. It won't be anything major."

Zach gave her his best bored look, crossed his arms over his chest and waited. For what, he wasn't sure. But he certainly knew he did not want any part of planning any kind of shower. Not wedding, not baby. Nothing. He designed and oversaw steel structures. He did not assemble froufrou place cards with little bells.

"Fine." The squeal of delight as Kayla jumped and wrapped her arms around him made him smile. "You knew I'd cave," he muttered.

"You always do with me." She eased back. "I'll forward you my spreadsheet once I'm in the air."

As she teetered away on spiky heels, her words registered. "Wait," he called after her. "Spreadsheet?"

"See you in a week," she yelled over her shoulder as she slid behind the wheel of her sleek luxury car.

"God, Zach, I'm so sorry." He turned to Ana's frustrated tone. "I hope she didn't leave because of Nate."

"Nate?"

"My ex-employee."

Zach shook his head. "Oh, no. She's on her way to the airport. Wait. *Ex*-employee?"

"I fired him."

Dumbfounded, Zach stared at Ana.

"Don't look at me like that," she insisted, turning to walk toward her office. "I won't accept anything less than professional behavior on the job."

Zach fell into step beside her. "Considering this is my site, too, I have some say. He whistled, Ana. Kayla wasn't offended and if she wasn't then there shouldn't be a problem."

She climbed up the rickety, wrought-iron steps, placed her hand on the knob and looked over her shoulder. "That I would've tolerated. Maybe. But as I got closer, his back was to me and he said some derogatory things about her *and* me that I'd rather not repeat. I won't accept demeaning comments toward women from my workers and neither should you."

Stunned at her matter-of-fact tone, Zach followed her into the air-conditioned office. "I don't accept anything less than professional behavior. But I would appreciate being brought in on such dealings that have any implication on this site."

With her back to him, she pulled open the top drawer of a file cabinet and began shuffling through papers before pulling one out and reading, still with her back to him. Not that he didn't appreciate the view.

"Hello? Are you listening?"

She peered over her shoulder. "I'll apologize for acting without consulting you, Zach, but I did what I thought was best."

"Your instincts were right. Just remember we're married to this project and like any good marriage, we should discuss major decisions."

"That's the second time you've mentioned this project being a marriage," she told him, her brow lifted in curiosity. "Being a world-famous bachelor, I'm surprised you know about marriages."

Damn. "Don't stereotype me, Ana. People aren't always what they seem or what the media make them out to be."

"You're right. Sometimes people are worse." She dropped the file on the edge of the desk and stepped toward him. "You haven't even thanked me for standing up for your sister, a woman whom I just met, by the way."

Zach took in her flushed face and the passion in her eyes. He didn't know what he wanted to do more, applaud her for standing up for his sister, kiss her senseless or throttle her for making him so damn confused lately.

Any woman who could match him in conversation and passion would surely match him in other, more fascinating areas. Perhaps that's why he couldn't get her off his mind. Beneath her cool exterior lurked an ember he wanted to fan to life.

"I'm just surprised you fired him without hesitation," Zach stated.

"That's because you know nothing about me, Zach." She looked back down at the papers on her desk. "If you did, you would know that I don't tolerate men showcasing their testosterone."

And that statement just solidified his previous assessment. Some jerk in her past had given her every reason in the world to be bitter toward the entire male gender, at least on a personal level.

"Anastasia, since we're going to be together on an almost daily basis for months, I think we better clear some things up real fast." Zach paused, waiting for her wounded eyes to come back up and meet his. "That chip on your shoulder has got to go. There's no way to work this long together and not have personal involvement on some level. If you have something to say to me, stop dancing around the topic and just say it. I know you've had a bad experience. You've got distressed damsel written all over your face."

He waited for her to correct him or defend herself. But damn if the spunky woman didn't break into a smile. The pointer just clicked upward a notch on the Ana Admiration Chart.

"Are you finished analyzing me?" she asked with a tilt of her head. "You may be used to flaunting your million-dollar smile at women and having them swoon at your feet, but don't look for me to get involved with you on anything other than a professional level. I have no secret past that you need to worry yourself with, nor am I a— What did you call me? A distressed damsel? Do you need an excuse to ride to a lady's rescue, Zach? Well, ride on. I'm not interested."

She advanced even closer. Zach refused to step back. He wanted to see those amber flecks in her green eyes. He wanted to breathe in that hint of floral fragrance that probably came from the shampoo she had used in all that hair—he didn't see her as a perfume spritzer. He wanted to watch her mouth as she matched him in this interesting conversation.

These sensations he was feeling and the head games he was playing with himself were certainly nothing he'd ever experienced on a job site before.

Damn, she was the sexiest little thing. He couldn't recall a woman getting in his face, demanding attention from him that was in no way a sexual come-on.

Purposeful or not, he was beyond turned on.

He had a feeling that the more he hung around Miss Anastasia Clark, the more fascinated he'd be.

"I've worked with men my whole life," she continued, "so I'm immune to charm. There's no come-on line you could throw my way that I haven't repelled before. So if your intention is to try your playboy style on me, you're wasting energy that would be put to better use on some busty socialite."

Yup. She was definitely going to be fascinating.

"Feel better?" he asked, not even bothering to hold back a smile.

Her brows drew together. "What?"

"Do you feel better since you put me in my place?"

Rolling her eyes, Ana laughed. "I doubt anyone has put you in your place, but I did want to let you know not to waste your smiles and flirtations on me. It wasn't professional, but you asked and I don't lie."

Zach rested his hip against her desk, in absolutely no hurry to leave. "What if I don't consider flirting with you a waste?"

She started to walk around her desk, but froze. "You're kidding, right? Can we get through this project without embarrassing ourselves?"

"Sure. On one condition." He waited until she turned fully to face him once again, and for some reason he opened his mouth without thinking the demand through. "I need your help planning my brother and soon-to-be sister-in-law's bridal shower."

Ana shook her head as if she hadn't heard him correctly. "Excuse me? Bridal shower? You starting a moonlighting career?"

He should've known she wouldn't make this easy for him. Perhaps, though, she would think he had a softer side and find him impossibly irresistible.

Yeah, right. With the smirk on her face, she was happy to have ammunition with which to make fun of him.

Yes, Ana was the perfect distraction to keep Melanie out of his mind.

"My sister is in charge, but she had to leave suddenly." And why was he explaining all of this to her? Since when did he ask to be mocked? "She asked me to help."

With a quirk of her arched brow, Ana eyed him. "So why are you sucking me into this? I've never been married."

He laughed. "You're a woman."

"So glad you noticed," she said dryly.

"Oh, I noticed." His eyes traveled down her fit body, unable to stay in one specific spot because she was just so...amazing. "I've noticed a lot about you."

She didn't cross her arms over her chest like most women would've. Ana kept her hands to her sides and actually tilted her head and rolled her eyes as if he was boring the life out of her. God, she had a strong backbone. How could he not find that attractive?

"Should I be flattered you're lumping me in with the other lucky ladies in your life?" she asked.

Zach chuckled. "Oh, Anastasia, you're definitely nothing like the ladies in my life, I assure you. You stand out all on your own."

Her eyes widened, her nostrils flared. "Can we get back to when you were begging for my help? My heart can't take all these romantic lines."

Begging? If he wasn't careful, she *would* have him begging.

Zach stared into her eyes, which wasn't hard considering she was nearly as tall as he was. What had made her so hard, so bitter? This wasn't about the project.

Even though he told himself it wasn't his problem, he couldn't help but wonder what it would take to make her warm up to him. He didn't want to be her shrink; he wanted to be her lover.

"Kayla's emailing me a to-do list," Zach explained. "What do you say we meet for dinner later and discuss the shower plans and the project?"

"You've got to be kidding me!" Ana exclaimed with a laugh. "You expect me to go on a date with you to help with a bridal shower to which I know neither party getting married? Is this how you normally get women?"

"Forget it." He wasn't going to beg or show weakness, no matter how much he needed help with this shower. He had no doubt Kayla's list would be detailed and lengthy, but he'd do it on his own. "And don't flatter yourself. I wasn't asking you for a date. It was business."

Let her stew on that.

"Business?" Ana seemed to think about her options. "Fine. I'll meet you at Hancock's at six. It's the only restaurant I've tried since I've been here and I know the food's good. If you're one minute late, I'm leaving."

He stepped closer, so close she tipped her head back to look into his eyes. "I'll pick you up at the condo you're renting. My assistant will have your address. I'll make reservations and tonight, Ana, you'll try something different."

"I'm not looking for different," she insisted.

Zach took her bare, slender shoulders in his hands and hauled her against his chest. "Neither was I."

Her eyes dropped to his lips. "You wouldn't."

"Timing's wrong," he muttered, hating himself for being a gentleman. "Just consider this your warning for when it's right."

The pulse beneath the sun-kissed skin on her neck pounded almost as hard as his own. Her tongue darted out to moisten her lips and he knew she was aroused. Welcome to the club.

The chirp of a cell attached to Ana's hip startled him. He stepped back, giving her a chance to answer.

Her hand shook as she jerked the phone from the holder. "Hello."

In a split second, her face went from passionate and curious to pale and stiff. "I'm busy right now."

Interesting. Zach was just grateful he wasn't on the receiving end of that icy voice. No, he was just fine being on her steamy side.

Which just went to prove his point. She wasn't immune to his charms like she insisted. The brittle, professional tone she used on him was nothing like now. At least when she spoke to him, there was heat in her voice. There was passion in her arguments.

"I will get back with you when I can. I'm working."

She disconnected the call, clipped the phone back on her hip, keeping her eyes averted from him for a minute.

Zach wondered who could get her so upset with a thirty-second call, but someone had and in the process had taken away the meager progress he'd made in chiseling away at her secure walls.

"Everything okay?" he asked, growing uncomfortable with her silence.

She glanced up at him, still void of any emotion he'd just seen in her eyes moments ago. "Fine," she snapped. "Now, as I told my father, I need to get to work."

Her father. He obviously didn't hold a special place in his little girl's heart. A pang of hurt settled in his chest at the ever-present memories of his own father.

Zach shook off the morose thought, not wanting to delve into his own past when he had the present and the future to concentrate on. All he wanted was to make this project run on schedule, within budget and be the most brilliant structure Victor Lawson had ever laid eyes, and money, on.

Getting the fiery Miss Anastasia Clark into his bed would be an added perk. And she would be there.

Unable to resist touching her smooth, heated skin once more, and because he wanted to replace that icy glaze in her eyes with anything else, Zach ran a fingertip down her cheek until her eyes locked on his.

He offered her a grin, holding her chin until the corners of her mouth eased up just a notch. "See you at six." Zach released her and headed for the door. "Oh, and don't wear your tool belt, Anastasia."

Three

Dressed and ready, Ana stood on the balcony of her condo overlooking the ocean. She loved the coast. Too bad all her jobs weren't in a sunny climate with the smell of the ocean to accompany her to work every day.

Most of her work took her from her Midwest home either farther west or north. Florida was certainly a place she could get used to. Building lavish, multimillion-dollar resorts was another thing she could get used to. Her company normally dealt with businesses or hotels and some smaller-scaled resorts, but no job compared to what she had going on now.

There was the day spa in Colorado that had left an impact because she had built it for post-cancer patients to not only receive treatments, but to get some much-needed pampering during their recovery time. That had left a special place in her heart.

And now Victor's resort would also leave an emotional impact.

She checked her watch once again. Zach had two minutes

before he was late. Typical chauvinist. Men like him thrived on the fact that women waited on them. And they expected their women to gasp with delight when they showed up at the door with an elaborate bouquet or expensive bottle of wine. As if that's all it took to get *her* into bed.

No, thanks. She wasn't the type to sigh, nor was she that easy to get into bed. Considering she'd never gone to bed with a man, she certainly wasn't going to start with Zach Marcum. He'd probably think being a virgin at twenty-eight was unheard of, but she was living proof. If her skirt-chasing father hadn't turned her off to intimacy, the gossip and stories she'd heard from her own mostly male crew over the years would surely have done the trick.

Besides, Zach was already getting more than he deserved. He was so used to women jumping through hoops for him at a moment's notice, and here she was following orders like a good little puppy. That was it. She would not, she vowed as she watched the whitecaps roll onto the beach, follow him into the bedroom. Handsome, sexy, impossibly charming. Yes, he was all that and so much more, but she had willpower. She'd survived this long in a workforce full of good-looking men. Surely she could work a few months with one drop-dead gorgeous playboy.

The heavy knock on her door jarred her from her thoughts. Cursing the jittery nerves deep in her belly, Ana smoothed a hand down her bright blue dress. She'd packed several dresses for this trip, certainly not with the hopes of going on a date, business or otherwise, but because she knew Victor Lawson liked to throw parties and show off his Star Island home and she would be expected to attend. But the dress she wore tonight wasn't fancy. Just a simple, fitted cotton tank. Though the dress showed off her slender, fit body, it did little to give her any of the feminine curves she wished she had. She was and always had been plain, simple…boring.

She strode through her condo and opened the door before she changed her mind.

Zach's swift intake of breath sent shivers through her. Zach Marcum shocked over a woman? Interesting. Maybe he didn't expect his women to do all the ogling.

"You look amazing."

Ana laughed. "You sound surprised. You did tell me to leave off my tool belt. Right?"

She didn't want to be affected by his heated gaze as it traveled from her freshly painted pale pink toes, up her bare legs to the rounded neckline of her dress.

"I just didn't expect…this," he said, bringing those dark chocolate eyes up to meet hers.

"It's just a plain dress, Zach." She had to lighten this tension. "I'm sure you've seen women in much fancier things."

"I have," he agreed, "but none of them could pull off simplicity like you can."

She felt a bit uneasy that this playboy was first speechless and then complimentary. Still she laughed, grabbed her key and slid it into her purse. "If you want me to put my sweaty tank and holey jeans back on, I can, but it comes with a hard hat and tool belt."

The smirk she'd come to know spread across his face. "While I admit you do look amazing in your work attire, I much prefer this sexy look."

Oh, dear. She may just sigh after all. Sexy? Now she saw why women fell so easily into his trap.

"If you're not too stunned at the fact that I do actually look like a woman off duty, shouldn't we go? You did make reservations, right?"

Zach brushed an auburn curl from her face, tucked it behind her ear. "Damn if I don't lose my head around you."

She didn't want to react to him, but her body couldn't help it. She tingled everywhere his eyes roamed. He might as well have caressed her with his big, strong hands. But that was all physical. There was no emotion deeper than that, which was fine. Ana could handle sexual attraction, but she sure as hell didn't intend to act on it.

Before this situation got even more uncomfortable, she ushered him out the door and headed toward the elevator.

When they slid into the elevator, Zach reached over and hit the Lobby button, then turned to her. "I have to say, not much makes me lose my train of thought. But that dress… It's like second skin."

"Did you think I'd actually show up wearing only sweat and my hammer?"

He closed his eyes. "Hold on. I'm getting a fantasy."

Ana couldn't help it; she laughed. "You're pathetic."

"Guilty." Zach shrugged. "Seriously, I owe you a nice dinner for standing up for my sister today."

Shocked, Ana smiled. "Is that all this is about?"

The elevator opened and Zach took hold of her elbow to usher her out.

"That and I need your help with planning this shower."

"You could've just given me the list of things Kayla wants you to do. There was no need for you to use up a free evening with me."

Now Zach laughed, forcing her attention back to the rich, soothing tone. He jerked her to a stop and forced her to face him.

"What's so funny?" she demanded.

"I never took you for a coward."

Ana wanted to wipe that knowing smirk off his face, but he was right. She was a coward on so many levels. He had no idea. She'd seen his playboy confidence, but when he'd conversed with his sister, his ego took a backseat to brotherly love and compassion. She didn't know what side of Zach she'd see next and the thought that she might just find every side attractive frightened her. She liked to be in control and around him, she wasn't.

"Call me what you want, but we both know you're so used to getting what you want that you made up this excuse to get me on a date." She tried her best to control her growing attraction to his bad-boy persona and heavy-lidded bedroom eyes. "I know your company has an impeccable reputation, but crossing the line into anything personal would be a mistake for both of us."

His smiling eyes grew dark, sexy. "You know as well as I do that that statement was just wasted breath. Deny all you want, but this mutual attraction is only going to cause more and more tension throughout the project if we ignore it."

She crossed her arms, lifted her chin and refused to get into such a personal discussion in a hotel lobby. She tugged free of his grasp on her arm and walked through the automatic doors and out onto the covered breezeway.

Thankfully the valet was absent, so Ana continued. "I'm not denying anything. I'm stating a fact that this project is my number one priority. I don't have time for a personal life, Zach."

Zach reached out, curled his hands around her bare shoulders and looked straight into her eyes. "This project is my number one priority, too, but I won't let it consume my downtime. And what we—yes, we—do together in our personal time has nothing to do with our working relationship."

This was an argument she knew she couldn't win, but once he found out she wasn't experienced, would he be as interested?

Zach led her toward a car she'd never seen the likes of before. The emblem read Bugatti, whatever that meant. Probably another word for "my car costs more than your yearly salary." Whatever the type, it was parked in a no-parking zone. Of course, the valets wouldn't dare move the superexpensive vehicle.

After assisting her into the lavish car, Ana settled into the soft leather seats as Zach slid in behind the wheel. When he didn't start the car immediately, Ana glanced over.

"Something wrong?" she asked.

He stared out the windshield, squinting against the sharp sunlight. "I'm beginning to think so."

Confused, she waited for him to elaborate, but the silence continued for several long moments.

"This is going to get complicated." He turned to her. "Whether we ignore the sexual tension or not. You and I are going to get complicated."

Ana didn't know how to respond. This level of sexual tension wasn't something she knew much about, but she had a gut-wrenching feeling she was about to find out sooner rather than later.

Blowing out a breath, Zach reached out and brushed her hair over her shoulders, his palm settled on the curve of her shoulder. "I'm up for the challenge. Are you?"

Could he hear the thumping in her chest? Honesty. She had to remain honest with him…and herself. This may be going faster and further than she'd intended, but she couldn't rein in her betraying emotions.

"Do I have a choice?"

He stroked a fingertip down her cheek. "No more than I do." Then he turned to start the car.

Mercy, how could she try to form immunity to this man when his touch was so gentle, his words so powerful? No wonder he had all the confidence in the world. There was no way any woman could resist his charm.

Was there anything sexier than a powerful, self-reliant man who made no qualms about the fact that he wanted you? And the man was so wrapped up in his family; that had to say something about character, didn't it? Oh, and let's not forget the way he looked on his big, black motorcycle. Not to mention the heavy-lidded bedroom eyes and dark stubble outlining a strong jaw.

For the duration of this project, they would be spending nearly every day together. Lord help her, this was going to be a very long year.

Four

The restaurant Zach took her to was certainly nowhere she'd ever choose to go herself. And though it was perfect, she'd never admit it to Mr. Overinflated Ego.

As the maître d' showed them to their reserved table, Ana took in the decor. Lush tropical plants in earthenware pots separated the dining tables, providing a cozy atmosphere. Low, soft lighting and one entire wall with a trickling waterfall made for a relaxing, intimate experience—just what she needed.

Ana slid into the curved booth in the corner beside the waterfall. Zach, too, slid in…right up to her side.

She eyed him with a quirk of her brow. "Do you plan on staying this close while we're eating?"

Beneath dark lashes and heavy lids, Zach returned her gaze. "At the first opportunity, I plan to get a lot closer."

Ana stared back into those deep, molasses-colored eyes. "Do you have a physical attraction to every woman you encounter?" she mocked.

"Not at all. I won't lie and say I've been a saint, but I also won't apologize for being honest and letting you know where I stand."

"Honesty is something I certainly appreciate, but I have to say, I don't trust easily."

He nodded. "You'll trust me. Maybe not now, but when it counts."

Oh, Lord. Did he mean…? Flirting was one thing, but his tone was so serious, so final. Sex was obviously something that came easily to Zach—or so the tabloids hinted at—so this conversation was probably only uncomfortable for her.

How had she lost control of this situation? Losing control of anything at all around Zach Marcum was not a smart move. She should be a pro at dealing with playboys considering all the self-proclaimed Casanovas on the job site. Unfortunately she'd never been on the receiving end of one's affections.

She turned in the booth, facing him fully. "Zach, we are nothing more than business associates and I'm helping you plan a wedding shower. That's just about as personal as I've gotten with anyone. Ever. Trust is an issue with me, but not one I care to fix."

Zach leaned down to her ear and whispered, "You don't have to do anything. I'll take care of fixing your trust issues."

His warm breath sent shivers throughout her body. Oh, man. This guy was good.

Too good. Too…rehearsed, like he'd said this before.

The waiter—thank you, God—chose that moment to come over. Ana ordered her dinner, but whatever Zach ordered was lost on her. She was too busy trying to figure out how to get ahold of this conversation, this man.

Once they were alone again, Ana shut out the romantic ambiance of the upscale restaurant, and the sexy, powerful man sitting within touching distance, and cut to the point.

"Why are you trying so hard?" she demanded. "You could surely have any woman you want."

Those bedroom eyes sparkled. "Not every woman."

The heat in his tone said more than his words.

Okay, so this wasn't a safe path to travel down.

"What list did Kayla give you for the shower?"

Zach grinned at her complete change of subject. "I need to form a seating chart and figure out the menu."

Much safer ground. "Sounds easy enough."

He eyed her. "You haven't seen the list of guests. There are specifics beside each name. Certain people can't be seated with each other, and the women with the children should be seated closest to the door for bathroom breaks."

Ana couldn't help but laugh at this high-profile mogul discussing wedding showers, seating charts and toddler potty rituals.

"It will be fine. I promise," she assured him, patting his arm. "But first, let's start with something less scary. The menu."

Zach nodded. "That I can handle. Steak and chicken are always basics."

"This is a bridal shower with women," she reminded him. "We like something less…masculine."

"You just ordered steak," he reminded her.

Ana shrugged. "I always have a huge appetite."

His eyes traveled down to her waist and back up. "You don't look like it. So what should we have? Carrot sticks and dip?"

His mocking tone and the little glint in his eye kept her smiling. Joking she could handle. It was the bedroom talk that gave her a problem.

"What time of the day is Kayla having the shower?" she asked.

The waiter came back, dropping off their drinks and

complimentary bread. Ana took a sip of her water and relaxed into the buttery leather booth.

"She said mid-afternoon. Two or three."

"Okay, so let's make this fun." Ana plotted quickly in her head. "What about a spin-off of an ice cream social? The shower will be after the guests have already eaten lunch, so various desserts would be perfect for women, and ice cream will be a hit with the kids that have to come along."

Zach turned a bit more in the seat, slid his arm along the back of the booth and offered her one of his killer smiles. "Keep going."

Pride flooded through her. Why she wanted to impress this man with plans for his sister-in-law-to-be's wedding shower was beyond her. Actually she just wanted to help out because he'd looked so completely lost when Kayla had dumped this on him.

And it was a good thing she'd stepped in when she did. Steak and chicken? She simply couldn't envision wealthy, beautiful socialites in vibrant sundresses, probably with floppy hats, gnawing on a T-bone.

"We should have this outside." Ana shook her head as the ideas swirled around. "No, make it somewhere that could be inside and out. We want them to mingle, chat and enjoy the celebration. Plus the ice cream would need to be out of all this blistering heat."

Zach held up a hand. "Isn't this a shower? Aren't the women supposed to sit around, sigh over the rock on Tamera's hand and play silly games?"

Ana shrugged. "I suppose if she wants a traditional, boring shower. Is your brother marrying someone boring?"

He chuckled. "Not at all. And knowing her and my sister, they will love this idea."

"Feel free to take the credit for it and be a hero," Ana said, reaching for a piece of warm, buttery bread.

"Why? It wasn't my idea."

She tore off the end piece and shoved it into her mouth. "They don't need to know a virtual stranger came up with plans for something so intimate and personal."

He eased a bit closer. Close enough now she could see the black slivers in his dark chocolate eyes.

"You're not a stranger, Ana."

The piece of bread she was holding slid from her grasp and fell onto the stark white linen tablecloth. She wanted to blame her slippery hands on the glazing from the bread, but honestly, Zach's warm breath combined with his intense stare had her all but trembling.

"Zach, you're not getting me into bed."

One corner of that sultry mouth kicked up. "Is that what I'm trying to do?"

"Aren't you? We can pretend you're flirting or just being yourself and I can giggle and bat my eyelashes at you like a good little tease…or we can skip all that nonsense and get to the heart of this tension between us."

He lifted one of her escaped auburn curls and tucked it behind her ear. "It's called chemistry. Not tension. Tension makes people uncomfortable. I'm perfectly fine."

"That's because you're used to throwing your charm out and having women latch on to it so you can drag them back to your lair."

Zach threw his head back and laughed. Ana waited, with very little patience, to see just what was so funny. If he even attempted to deny that he was a playboy, she feared she'd stab him with her salad fork.

"Ana, I'm not a Neanderthal," he said in a low, still chuckling voice. "I don't drag women anywhere they aren't willing to be. Don't get your back all up because you're angry over your attraction to me."

Maybe she'd have to use that salad fork after all.

"Your ego and your comments are out of control," she hissed. "I won't deny I'm attracted to you, but I also don't need to act on every urge I have. And I don't have time for games."

Ana tried to scoot over into her own personal space. Zach must've thought she was making a dramatic exit because he grabbed her arm and whispered in her ear, "I'll apologize for my comments, but you know I'm right."

Ana kept her gaze on the roll she'd dropped onto the table, trying her hardest to avoid turning her head and looking him in the eye. He was so close that if she turned even the slightest, their faces would touch.

The devil on her shoulder wanted to know if that would be so bad. The angel on the other shoulder must be asleep because she didn't say a word. Or maybe she was just stunned speechless because Zach's large hand encircled her entire bicep in a warm, gentle hold.

Ana closed her eyes. "I can't do this. Seriously, Zach. I can't even pretend that we'll be more than business associates because I won't play a tease and I won't lie to you. Please stop pushing me into giving you something I can't."

His thumb stroked over the curve of her shoulder. "That was never my intent, Anastasia."

Now she did turn to meet his gaze, leaving their lips barely a whisper apart. "What was your intent?" she whispered.

Other than his lips settling over hers in a possessive, yet tender way, Zach didn't touch her. Ana didn't want to respond to those lips, but how could she not? Why did she have to deny what her body so desperately craved, ached for?

It was so easy to give into the gentleness. She'd never known such a delicate manner could be possessed by a man like Zach.

Ana wasn't one for PDA, but they were well hidden by the strategically placed potted palms. Even though kissing in public was never something she would've done before meeting Zach, she was discovering there were a lot of things she hadn't considered before meeting Zach.

With a sigh and a tingle streaming through her body, Ana leaned in just slightly. Enough to let Zach know she wanted this. Still, he didn't touch any more than her lips and Ana knew, without a doubt, he was letting her decide how far and how intense this kiss would be.

He tilted his mouth just a bit, easing her lips open. She'd given him the go-ahead with that little sigh and by leaning into him. A light, feathery touch slid across her jawline. His fingertips.

Chills popped up over her entire body. And before she could comprehend another thought, Zach eased back.

"My intent is to show you how desirable you are and that not every man takes advantage of women."

Ana opened her eyes, swallowed hard. "Maybe not, but not every man has good intentions."

His fingertips continued to stroke her jawline. "There's nothing wrong with giving in to your needs, your passion. I'm a patient man, Anastasia, and I believe you're well worth the wait."

Great, now her chills had chills. At his declaration—or was it a threat—Ana knew she was fighting a losing battle.

Did he have a clue about her inexperience? Did she bring it up? And how did one start the ball rolling with a topic like this?

Though she didn't want to admit it, Ana knew she'd long since lost control. And much to her surprise, she didn't care.

Five

Zach sped through the palm-lined Miami streets. When darkness had fallen over the party town, Zach had taken off on one of his favorite motorcycles to clear his head, taste a bit of freedom he refused to let go of and work through whatever problems were plaguing his mind.

And right now all three of those scenarios revolved around one sexy, stubborn forewoman.

Zach eased his Harley to a stop on the beach side of the street. The full moon beamed right onto the whitecaps of the waves rolling into shore.

After he'd dropped Ana off at her hotel, he'd needed to do some major regrouping. There had been almost an innocence, a naïveté about her tonight. He hadn't missed the way her hands shook when he'd scooted closer, the quivering in her voice when he'd stroked her bare shoulder.

The hitch in her breath when he'd finally kissed her. He'd never taken so much time before kissing a woman before.

Never had to rein in his emotions when all he wanted to do was act on them.

And to say she had a hidden passion would be a drastic understatement. Ana had leaned into him; she'd given up control and handed it over to him in the span of one audible sigh.

There wasn't a doubt in his mind she would be just as passionate in a private, intimate setting. A woman with such fire and determination for everything that she came across in life would surely match his own desires.

Ana may be powerful, controlling and in charge in her business, but he intended to pull all of that from her when he got her into bed. He'd already had a glimpse of how easily Ana gave into her urges.

One part of him wished he could pinpoint the exact reason he wanted Ana so much; the other part didn't give a damn about the reason. She was beautiful and unattainable—a challenge tailor-made for him.

Zach's cell vibrated in his pocket. He reached in, checked the ID and sighed as he thumbed the green button.

"Melanie."

"Can I come over?"

Zach felt the immediate tightening in his chest. Here was the woman he'd married, the one he thought he'd love forever. The one who'd left without a backward glance...until now, when she realized her mistake.

"Mel, you left me. I don't give second chances."

"I made a mistake. Can't we just talk?"

As much as Zach wanted to, he couldn't, wouldn't give her the opportunity to destroy him again. He wouldn't give that to any woman.

"I have to go."

Zach disconnected the call and shoved his cell back in his pocket before staring out onto the whitecaps ebbing and flowing along the beach. He couldn't help but think of his wedding day and the brief months of wedded bliss…followed by the whole nightmarish moment that he'd just as soon forget. And he would, just as soon as Melanie quit calling and texting him.

Yes, his ex had done something to him that damaged him, but he also took some blame for the disaster. If he hadn't left himself so vulnerable, so open, he wouldn't have been so hurt when she left him for one of his so-called friends.

Cliché, yes. But Zach was moving forward, getting on with his life and making the most of every moment of his freedom and bachelorhood.

He refused to be analyzed, or to even admit to himself that he'd thrown himself in the path of every single woman he could since his divorce. So what if he wanted to enjoy the company of a woman without the baggage of a relationship?

And if he wanted to spend the next few months entertaining Ana, then that's what he would damn well do.

But if he didn't curtail his desire for Ana, the entire crew would know. This physical pull he felt toward the forewoman had to remain under wraps…preferably under covers.

Working with such a juxtaposed woman every day for months wouldn't be a hardship, but it would be trying on his patience. Patience was certainly not something he'd ever had, but he knew if he wanted to be with Ana, and he did, he'd have to dig deep to find that most elusive quality.

He also figured he'd have to take this seduction plan slower than he would've liked. Ana was hesitant to give into her desires. He couldn't quite pinpoint why, but whatever secrets she hid in her past were her business. All he wanted was her now, in the present.

Forget the past, don't think about the future—his mantra for the past couple years. He'd lived any way he'd wanted, saw whom he pleased. On some insane level he should be happy his ex-wife had left him for another man because he could do whatever the hell he wanted.

But he found himself wanting Ana on a physical level that was starting to consume each and every thought.

Would Ana be willing to step around that wall of defense she'd built around herself? If not, was he really willing to risk the possibility of another rejection? For intimate time with Ana, absolutely. Hadn't he steeled his heart? He could certainly handle an intimate relationship with Ana.

Relationship? No, he didn't do those. Flings? Certainly. But he had a gut feeling Miss Ana was not a fling-type girl.

So he was back to asking himself the relationship question. Would he—?

Zach cursed as he looked skyward and saw the dark clouds closing in over the full moon. He started his engine back up and headed for home as the first raindrop landed on his forearm.

He didn't consider it a coincidence that the rain interrupted his thoughts just as they were about to venture into a territory he wasn't quite ready for. Fate was telling him something.

No way was he at a point in his life when he wanted to explore deeper feelings. And honestly, he didn't know if he'd ever be ready to give any woman, even Ana, something more than his body. And that was just fine with him.

A week had passed since Zach had made a pass at her in any way. Oh, they'd worked throughout the day at the site, but he was all business, all the time.

As she stood in front of the bathroom mirror in her condo suite wearing only a fluffy towel and light makeup, Ana felt the nerves flutter in her stomach. Tonight was anything but work.

Victor Lawson was hosting a party, so of course she was not only invited, she was expected to attend. Zach would be there which made Ana take special care while fixing her dark auburn curls. The South Florida humidity made her hair unruly, so she pulled the large-barreled curling iron through it to smooth the ends under and pulled it back into a low, loopy bun.

She gave her hair and makeup one final check before she made her way to the closet to choose between the few dresses she'd brought to Miami. She fingered the hangers, eyeing the ice-blue cocktail dress, the short emerald halter-style or maybe the bold, purple strapless.

The emerald halter won. It was comfortable, light and flirty. Plus the color really accented her eyes which would be great because she didn't wear that much eye makeup.

Ana chose her undergarments with care, but not because she planned on anyone else seeing them. Quite the contrary. Having sexy, feminine, lacy lingerie gave her an extra boost of confidence. And she knew attending a high-class party with numerous Alpha male types—Victor, Cole, Zach—she'd need all the confidence she could get.

Considering she had a meager bust, she decided to forgo the bra and donned a pair of black lace panties cut high on the hip. She slid the dress over her head and tied the chiffon straps around her neck.

Then she stepped into a pair of gold strappy heels.

Turning from side to side in front of the closet mirrors, Ana smiled. No way did she look like a construction worker now. If Zach thought he wanted the dirty, plain tank and jeans girl, wait until he caught sight of her inner vixen.

Make that the virginal vixen. Ana chuckled. Oxymoron, anyone?

After touching up her lip gloss, she slid the slender tube into her small, gold clutch at the same time a heavy knock sounded at her door.

She glanced through the peephole, not surprised to see Zach, looking as gorgeous and sexy as ever, on the other side. Of course, she wasn't going to tell him he looked gorgeous or sexy. Those were details that he already knew about himself.

Besides, she had a feeling he'd had enough women to stroke his ego.

But she would make him just a bit miserable tonight. After all, she'd been miserable since he'd laid that talented mouth on hers.

She smoothed a shaky hand down the front of her short, flowing dress and opened the door. Zach's wide eyes raked over her from head to toe, twice, before settling on her glossy lips. The look on his face made her grin and do a little happy dance inside because she'd chosen the right outfit for the impact she wanted.

"I'm glad I came to give you a ride," he said in a raspy, sexy voice. "If you walked into that party alone, you'd be eaten alive by every eligible bachelor there. And probably some married men, too."

Ana conjured up that inner vixen and cocked a hip to the side as she slid a hand up the door. "What makes you think I want to ride with you? Maybe I wanted to walk into Victor's party alone."

Those chocolate eyes grew darker as he looked at her. "You keep taunting me, sweetheart, you'll have to face the consequences."

A flicker of arousal mixed with fear crept through her, but she kept her stance, refusing to let him get one up on her just because she was inexperienced. And why was she purposely antagonizing this tiger? Was she finally done being one of the guys? Did she really want to take a chance on letting Zach have his way with her?

Good Lord, she had come so far. She was actually enjoying this banter with Zach.

"If you don't want to be taunted," she said, smiling, "keep your distance."

In one swift step, he closed the gap between them, snaked an arm around her waist and brought his face within an inch of hers. "I've tried. Even when you're not with me, you're filling my thoughts. What do you suppose we do about that?"

Suddenly not feeling so confident, Ana placed her hands on the hard planes of his broad chest. "I say we get to the party before Victor wonders why we're late."

Zach's eyes roamed down the V of her halter. "Once he sees you, he'll not only know why we were late, he'll completely understand."

Ana gave him a not-so-gentle shove, pushing Zach away. "Simmer down, lover boy. Let me grab my key and purse. I hope you don't think I'm straddling one of your flashy bikes for this."

Zach cocked his head and grinned. "I'm pure class tonight, Anastasia. I brought my new Camaro."

"Camaro? I thought all you flashy playboys liked expensive, foreign cars."

He shrugged. "We like all kinds of toys and I have my fair share of foreign models, but I always wanted a Camaro when I was in high school and we couldn't even afford a beat-up car, much less something flashy. The second I laid my eyes on this new model, black of course, with a sharp set of rims, I knew it was mine."

Ana studied him. "Are you telling me you didn't have a car as a teenager?"

Zach stepped a bit farther into her bedroom as she gathered her things. "No. Cole and I shared the car our mom drove before she and my father passed away, but we didn't have our own. Poor Kayla, she never had one until she got her first job in college and bought one."

Ana wanted to know more about this surprising childhood of Zach's. How had the three siblings gone from one car and no money to numerous lavish homes and a multimillion-dollar business?

"I appreciate having a Camaro now, though," he said with a

menacing smile. "I wouldn't have been man enough to handle all that engine when I was younger."

She laughed and stepped toward him in a silent gesture to leave. "And you think you're man enough now to handle it?"

His smile slipped and his heavy-lidded eyes held her in place. "I'm man enough to handle anything."

Unsure of how to respond, Ana retrieved her clutch and key from the dresser. After sliding the key into her purse, she turned, ready to face the den full of lions. Please God, she prayed, don't let me be the only woman at this party. Then again, with a man like Victor Lawson, there were probably dozens of women to dangle off his arms.

"Who's that?" Zach asked, nodding to the picture on the dresser.

"My grandfather and my mother." She didn't want him to come any farther into her room. Her pictures were personal, just like her life. "Ready?"

He nodded and extended his elbow out to escort her. Looping her arm around his crisp, black dress shirt, she immediately felt the heat permeating from him. Heaven help her, the night had just begun.

As they approached the elevator, he straightened his arm and laced their fingers together. The gesture was intimate for her, probably not so much for someone like famous ladies' man Zach Marcum.

They rode down in silence and made their way across the marbled floor of the lobby and out into the balmy Miami night. Onlookers wouldn't think twice about the dressy couple, hand in hand, getting into a flashy car for a date.

Looks could be deceiving. That was something she knew firsthand.

Zach opened the passenger-side door of his Camaro and assisted her in before closing the door. As if she needed another one of her senses honing in on him, the masculine, crisp scent from his cologne, which somehow mixed perfectly with the new-car scent, completely enveloped her just as the plush leather seat did. The man himself may as well wrap those big, strong arms around her. The impact of her current surroundings was just as effective.

Before she could analyze her cozy ride, Zach slid in beside her and brought the engine to life.

"I was going to bring the 'Vette, but I only keep the top down and I figured you wouldn't appreciate your hair getting blown everywhere."

Ana crossed her legs and laughed. "For something like this, that was a safe assumption. Normally, though, I'd love it. I'm not too worried if my hair is perfect or if my lipstick is always in place. With me, what you see is what you get."

Oops, bad choice of words. She knew it even in that split second before Zach's eyes darted to the side to give her a visual caress.

"I haven't got anything yet, have I?"

His words may have been teasing; his tone was anything but. This man wasn't known for his somewhat wild lifestyle for nothing. He knew what he wanted and he never let anything get in his way.

And right now, he had his eye on the prize. She may as well parade around wearing nothing but a shiny red bow.

Six

The second they entered Victor Lawson's lavish Star Island mansion, Zach was more than ready to throw a coat over Ana and usher her back to his car.

Every eye was on them—and he knew they weren't looking at him. The men were blatantly staring and the women were shooting invisible daggers. They had every reason to be jealous.

"Ah, two of my favorite people." Victor crossed the black marble floor from the back of the house to greet them. "I'm so glad you made it. We have drinks, food, people. All the makings of a fantastic evening."

Zach eased a hand to the small of Ana's back. A petty claim he was staking, but he wanted the oglers to take note. Why he was so damned determined to show others how much he wanted her was beyond him. Hadn't he told his brother he was only interested in Ana in an intimate setting? He simply didn't share, that's all. No reason for him to analyze this situation into anything more than what it was. Ana was the perfect woman to occupy his nights.

"We were afraid we were going to be late," Zach stated, earning him a death glare from Ana. "I told her you'd understand."

Victor chuckled. "Absolutely."

"Your house is absolutely breathtaking, Victor." Ana offered the billionaire her sweetest, most sincere smile. "Thank you for the invitation."

Victor reached for her hand, brought it to his lips. "No thanks necessary, Anastasia. You are aiding in making my next hotel the most glamorous of all. It is I who should be thanking you."

Okay, that hand-holding had been going on a bit too long. Zach was ready to go Neanderthal until Victor glanced his way. An unspoken male conversation passed between them and then Victor nodded, grinned and released Ana's hand.

"I must go see to my other guests," Victor said. "If there's something you want and don't see it, ask one of the waitstaff to get it for you."

The second Victor walked away, Ana turned to Zach. "Don't you *ever* do that again."

"I didn't want him getting any ideas," he defended. "He's a single man who's more than popular with the ladies. I just wanted him to know you were off-limits."

"I'm off-limits to you as well," she whispered between gritted teeth before she turned and headed toward the back of the house where all the French doors lining the rear wall were open to the magnificent backyard.

Zach allowed her a few feet head start then casually followed. No way was he going to make a scene, especially at the home of the man who held a multimillion-dollar deal with his family's architectural firm.

Before Zach could step outside with Ana, Victor approached him once again.

"Is Kayla still out of the country?" he asked.

"Yes. I believe she's due back within the week. Did you ed to talk to her about the hotel?"

Victor shook his head. "No, nothing associated with busi-ss."

Zach didn't get a chance to reply. Victor had walked away d was already mingling with other guests.

Interesting. Victor wanted something personal with Kayla? n uneasy feeling formed low in his gut. He didn't like the oughts of that billionaire bachelor with Ana and he sure as ll didn't like the idea of him pawing at his sister.

But that was something he'd have to get Cole in on. There as no way his sweet, soft-spoken sister was going to have y dealings with Victor other than business.

Zach walked through the open French doors and out to the garden…if such an extravagant floral garden with aterfalls trickling into small ponds could be called a garden. he simple word seemed much too tame for the amazing enery.

Rich, throaty laughter floated through the air, sucker nching him deep in the gut. Ana. He'd know that laugh ywhere, but just how he would know was a mystery. She'd rtainly never laughed that sexily around him.

He spotted her a few feet away standing beside his twin other, Cole, and Cole's fiancée, Tamera. The women were niling and chatting while Cole nursed a longneck. No doubt e women were discussing the upcoming wedding.

Zach didn't know if he should stand back and take in the eauty of the smile Ana offered or if he should go save his other.

But like the magnetic force that seemed to draw him tely toward the stubborn, sexy woman, Zach found himself osing the gap and standing so close to Ana, his arm brushed rs. Even though she continued smiling, her body tensed, ivered.

"Glad you could make it," Cole stated, slapping him on the arm.

"Me, too," Zach replied, taking a bottle of imported beer from a passing waiter. "Tamera, you're looking beautiful as always. You're almost glowing you look so happy."

His soon-to-be sister-in-law beamed, slipping an arm around Cole's waist and leaning into him. "I have many reasons to be happy and they all revolve around this guy right here."

"I was just asking where they're getting married," Ana chimed in. "I'm surprised they're getting married at Cole's house."

"We didn't want anything unfamiliar or too out of the way for our closest family and friends." Tamera looked up to Cole, love radiating around them. "We plan on having a long reception and leaving for our honeymoon right after and we wanted a place for our family to stay overnight. Our house seemed perfect."

Ana smiled. "That sounds wonderful. Very intimate and personal."

Zach was certain if all this love, wedding and happily-ever-after talk proceeded much longer, he'd break out in head-to-toe hives. This was definitely not a topic he was comfortable with, nor did he want to hang around long enough to get comfortable with it. The moment would never come.

"Been by the site in the last couple days?" he asked Cole.

His twin nodded. "Matter of fact I ran by earlier today."

"The preparations are coming along ahead of schedule and the rest of Ana's crew arrived two days ago, so that will speed things along even more."

Tamera rolled her eyes. "Do we have to discuss work? We're all off, so let's just enjoy the party. I'm hungry, Cole. Let's go get a plate."

Cole eyed his brother, giving him the "we'll talk later"

ok. Zach chuckled as he took a long pull of his beer. Never, ver would a woman get that deep into his life that she called e shots on his next move. Just another reason love wasn't r him.

It was something he wished he would've known before his ife ran off with another man and then continued to haunt im because her affair didn't last.

But Zach was happy his brother and Tamera had found eir way back to each other and were now planning the edding of the year.

"Don't look so sour," Ana said, snapping him from his oughts. "If you want to talk shop, I'm all ears."

"A woman after my own heart," he joked.

A lopsided grin spread across her face. "I'm hardly after ur heart, Zach."

"That's good, considering I won't give it away again."

"Again?"

Dammit. Of all the times to bring up his most vulnerable oment.

"I was married before," he said casually. "Didn't last. She ants back together, I don't. End of story."

Ana rubbed a delicate hand up her arm and shook her head. ust another reason we're so different. Marriage is a huge eal. That's one of the reasons I never want to do it. There's o way a man would be what I need in a husband."

Interesting. "What do you want?"

She shrugged, clutching her tiny purse with both hands. t's not so much what I want as what I need. Faithfulness, yalty, stability, honesty. He'd have to put me first. I'm not ying spoil me and pamper me, I'm saying be attentive to y needs and know my desires."

If only she'd let him know her desires, he'd meet every ngle one of them. But he certainly wasn't vying for a slot in e husband category.

"Don't get me wrong," she went on, staring at all the

couples mingling hand in hand around the lavish ground
"I'm so happy when two people who are meant to be togeth
find that happiness. It's just not something I'll ever have. Bu
believe me, I'm not complaining."

The longer she talked and watched other people, the clear
it became she was lying. Oh, she may not know she was lyin
to herself, but she was. The longing in her eyes, the softness
her voice as she spoke of her requirements... Yes, Anastas
Clark wanted that fairy tale and one day she'd probably fir
it. The right man would come along and give her all of th
and more.

Zach didn't want to think about Ana with another man. N
when he hadn't even had a chance to explore that passion th
lurked inside of her.

"Oh, and a dog," she added.

"Excuse me?"

She turned her pale green eyes back to him. "I'd have 1
have a dog. If he loves animals, then that's a good sign he
caring and nurturing. Of course, in my work a dog isn't ver
practical, not with me traveling all over the country."

"Maybe when you meet your prince charming, you'll sett
into his castle and not travel anymore." Zach couldn't help b
grin as her eyes narrowed. "Then you can have all the dog
you want."

"I told you, I'm not settling down. I'm certainly not slowir
down anytime soon on my work, either. I love what I do, lov
my independence."

Even better. She wasn't looking for a commitment. Pe
fect.

"I see a client of mine," Zach told her. "I need to go say h
You're welcome to come with me."

She waved a hand through the air. "You don't need t
babysit me. Go, mingle. I'll come find you when I'm ready

Zach left Ana as she made her way toward one of th
numerous tiered food tables. He chatted with one client, an

en with many more previous clients his family's firm had
orked with.

After about an hour, Zach scanned the area for Ana but
d no luck in spotting her. Surely she wouldn't have left with
meone and not told him. He wandered back in through one
the seven French doors that led into the house. This set led
to the formal sitting room where more partygoers chatted.
o Ana.

Then he heard that sexy laugh.

His head darted around and he spotted that red hair, that
nerald dress, and his ever-present arousal smacked him in
e face. Jealousy soon followed as he watched her chat with a
an that Zach knew was married to a very sweet, unknowing
oman. The rich, middle-aged man smiled as he pushed a
ray strand of Ana's hair that had slipped from her bun.

Zach had never considered himself territorial before, but
ere was no way in hell he could let this go on. He had no
oubt Ana didn't have a clue the man she was talking to had a
ischievous gleam in his eye and had set his sights on her.

"Gabriel Stanley, nice to see you again," Zach said as
e approached, not affected one bit by the glare he'd just
ceived from the other man. "I saw your wife outside. She
oks wonderful. You two having another boy?"

Gabriel shoved his hands in his dress-pants pockets. "Yes.
e're having our third boy."

"How wonderful," Ana beamed, oblivious to the tension.
Congratulations. You didn't tell me that."

Zach nearly laughed. No, old Gabriel probably didn't tell
is prey he had a wife and family…. That would certainly put
damper on any affair he hoped to have with her.

"She looked a bit tired," Zach added. "You may want to
heck on her."

The muscle in Gabriel's jaw ticked. "Ana, it was a pleasure
meet you. Zach, see you around."

"Well, that was incredibly rude," Ana said once they were alone. "Why didn't you pee on me to mark your territory?"

Zach stood directly in front of her, staring into those eyes that were as mesmerizing as any emerald. "He's married."

"And?"

"He was flirting with you."

Ana grinned and patted him on the cheek. "You're cute when you're jealous. Almost makes me want to pursue that to see if those feelings are sincere."

"I'm not jealous," he insisted, though if that got another foot inside her stone wall, he'd own up to it. "Let's go."

She opened her mouth as if she wanted to argue, but closed it and nodded. "We should tell Victor goodbye."

"He's busy talking with guests. He won't mind if we slip out."

Giving her no other option, Zach took her hand and led her through the mansion and out onto the stone driveway where they waited for the valet to bring the car up.

Strained silence accompanied them back to her South Beach condo. He didn't want her to think of him as a jerk. After all, wasn't he supposed to be showing her a different side of men?

Wait a minute. Since when had his conquest gone from getting into her bed to showing her that he was genuinely interested in getting to know her? He didn't want a relationship by any means. Then again, if they were going to be together so much, he might as well work every angle to his advantage.

"Look, I'm sorry if you think I was rude to you back there." He cleared his throat. "But I won't apologize for being rude to Gabriel."

"Yeah, that sounded sincere."

Zach shot her a quick sideways glance. "I am sincere. And I'm not afraid to apologize when I know I'm wrong or I've hurt someone's feelings that I care about."

Her sharp intake of breath shocked him. He'd better clarify his statement.

"I know how you view men," he went on. "But we're not all bad and we're not all like Gabriel. Just because some men choose to enjoy women doesn't mean they are playing them. They may just be dating around, one at a time and having fun."

"Like you," she said.

Sitting this close, with her wearing so little, Zach had to reach out to touch her. He slid his hand across the console and rested it on her thigh. "Like me. I don't lie to women, ever. If I'm with someone, she knows where I stand on relationships and she also knows that she can trust me not to be with someone else while I'm with her."

"For some reason, I believe you."

And for some reason, he exhaled a breath he hadn't known he was holding. He wanted Ana to think of him as one of the good guys. He wanted to set the bar for her so when she did go out and realize she wanted that fairy tale, she wouldn't fall for any frogs.

Dammit. He was now thinking like a five-year-old little girl. He was a man, for crying out loud. He wasn't supposed to think of fairy tales and frogs.

Bottom line, he'd show her how a real man was supposed to treat a woman. And he could certainly do that without getting wrapped up in a relationship.

Seven

When Zach pulled up to her condo, she started to get out. "Thanks for the ride."

"I'll see you up."

She began to protest as he exited the car, but he quickly opened her door and extended his hand, leaving her no choice but to accept his gesture and follow. She wanted to get away from him, away from his overbearing antics. She was a grown woman, for heaven's sake and she could handle herself. Maybe she had liked being hit on at Victor's party—though the fact that Gabriel Stanley was married with a child on the way was a bit creepy and extremely wrong.

Zach told the valet that he'd be right back, then he slid an arm around her waist and escorted her inside to the elevator.

The he-man routine wasn't quite her style, but she couldn't help but feel humbled and a bit special because he'd come up to her when he thought she may be getting in over her head with a married man.

Either Zach had really high morals about fidelity or he wanted her all to himself.

Or, the most likely scenario, both. A part of her worried she was taking this flirting too far.

Ana flicked open her clutch as the elevator dinged on her floor. Zach's hand hadn't moved from her back and the heat radiating from him had probably put a hole right through her dress.

The simple affection made her heart flip, but she knew it was only because she wasn't used to seeing that side of a man. She was used to sweaty, grimy men working all day on sites. She hadn't been on a date in months and even then, it hadn't been anything special.

Zach took the key card from her and slid it into her door. She couldn't let him in. Not only did she fear her willpower would fizzle the second he stepped over that threshold and the door slammed behind him, but she couldn't let him see all of her personal things. No one ever saw all the items she carried with her from site to site. They were her sanctuary. When he'd questioned her earlier about her pictures, she'd panicked.

Zach opened the door, gesturing for Ana to step in ahead of him.

"Thanks again." She turned, holding her hand out for the key. "I'm sure I'll see you Monday."

Zach didn't turn the key over to her like she'd expected. He kept hold of it while his eyes roamed over her face, focusing on her lips.

"I've watched you all night," he told her in a softer, huskier voice. "Watched that creamy skin slide against your dress. Pieces of your hair dance around in the breeze. I've never practiced more restraint than I did tonight."

Control had to remain with her, she knew, or they would both make a decision they weren't ready for. "Don't, Zach. Just give me the key."

He laid the key in her upturned palm, only to cup the side of her face and stroke her bottom lip with his thumb. "You don't want me to go. If you're honest with yourself, you want to know what it would be like."

The "it" wasn't in question. And, yes, she had wondered, dreamed. But that didn't mean anything could or would happen. Though she knew exactly what he was talking about when he'd said he'd practiced self-restraint. God knew she was having to hold herself back right now.

She never thought she'd be at the point of restraint. She'd always assumed when she chose to take a lover, she would be so certain, all of her doubts would vanish. Yeah, so not the case. Not that she'd decided one hundred percent to take Zach as her lover, but she was inching closer and closer.

"We're so different, Zach."

He stepped closer. "Then why aren't you pushing me away?"

Because she couldn't form a coherent thought. Between his sultry words, that crisp scent of his cologne and his potent touch, Ana only knew her body was approaching flashpoint and was racked by an ache she hadn't felt before now.

"I'll go if you tell me to," he murmured a second before his lips came down onto hers.

Both arms came around her waist as he softly coaxed her lips open with his tongue. With her dress low-cut in the back, Zach's rough palms slid over her smooth skin, proving once again how opposite they were…yet how amazing he felt.

He pressed her against his body as one hand snaked up beneath her hair and massaged her neck.

With all the assaults on her body at once, Ana hadn't even noticed Zach had backed her farther into the foyer until the door clicked shut, closing out the light from the hallway.

Ana pulled back, her hands clutching his hard biceps. A soft glow from the living room filtered around them, but the half-wall kept most of the light out.

"Zach," she said breathlessly, "I can't. We can't."

Zach's eyelids were heavy, his lips moist and swollen, his breathing erratic. "Don't be scared," he whispered as he eased her back against the wall and covered her mouth once again.

Scared happened long ago. Now she was downright terrified. Certainly not of him, but of herself for wanting something, craving something she had no control over.

Ana wrapped her arms around his neck and pressed her aching body to his. The tie behind her neck came free with ease as Zach gave the knot a gentle tug. The soft material slid down, stopping where their bodies were joined.

Zach eased back, breaking their kiss for a moment. They both looked down as the top of her halter dress slid away from her breasts.

"Breathtaking," he whispered.

Ana didn't know what to say, what to do. "Zach…"

"Shh." He laid a finger to her lips. "I won't hurt you."

She pushed just a bit more against his chest before he could claim her tingling lips again. "I've never done this before. And as much as I'd like to give in, I just can't."

Zach stared at her, as if only just registering her words. Then slowly he pulled her straps back up, tied them around her neck with shaky hands.

Ana didn't take her eyes off him as he straightened her dress. Embarrassment and shame filled her. "I didn't mean to tease you or to let this get out of hand."

He stepped back, shoved his hands into the pockets of his dress pants. "I don't know what to say."

Feeling the need for security, Ana wrapped her arms around her waist and glanced down to the floor. "It's okay. You can just go and we'll pretend this night never happened. This was my fault for letting you in."

"Nobody lets me do anything." His husky voice enveloped

her. "I wanted to come in with you, Anastasia. Nothing could've kept me out."

She couldn't look at him, didn't want to see the disappointment in his eyes. Since when had his feelings and what he thought of her really mattered? This was precisely why she didn't get involved, on any level, with men. Her emotions weren't too far below her steel surface and it never took much for them to slip out.

Zach's fingertip slid beneath her chin and tipped her face up. "Look at me."

As much as she wanted to avoid him, she knew the sooner she cooperated, the sooner he would leave and she could get past this awkward moment.

Ana lifted her gaze, but instead of finding anger or disappointment, she discovered a passionate, caring look she'd never expected in Zach's eyes.

"Why are you ashamed?" he asked. "I'm surprised, yes, but I'm even more impressed. I knew you were strong, independent, but I had no idea just how vulnerable you were."

She straightened her shoulders. "I'm not vulnerable or ashamed."

He stroked the pad of his thumb over her lips. "Don't lie to me or yourself. You think I'm disappointed, so you're ashamed you lost control. You're also vulnerable or you would've let go long ago. You're afraid of getting hurt. Who hurt you in your past, Ana? Who put this worry, this doubt in you?"

The burn began in her eyes, her nose, then her throat. When tears threatened to spill down her cheeks, she closed her eyes and turned away to break free of his mesmerizing touch.

"Leave," she whispered. "Just…leave."

"I would never force you, would never make you feel pressured. But I won't let go of this attraction between us and neither will you." Zach reached for the door, pulled on the knob. "I'm a patient man when I see something I want.

I'll wait for you, Anastasia. Because I want you more than anything I've wanted in a long time. That's new for both of us and something we'll have to get used to."

Before she could say anything else, he opened the door and left.

Ana stood bone weary against the wall opposite the large entryway mirror. She nearly didn't recognize herself. Dress sagging from the loose knot Zach tied, mouth swollen, flushed cheeks, mass of curls falling loose from her clip to hang around her face and shoulders.

She looked like a woman who'd been through a battle. Had she ever. And all this time she'd not wanted him to come in to her condo for personal reasons.

A giggle escaped her. Well, at least he didn't see her family pictures she kept on her nightstand. Though him seeing all her family she'd once had and now longed for would've been a whole lot easier to deal with than letting him in on her intimate, private secret that she'd never been with a man.

Now he was more determined than ever to get close to her. What had she done? She had to tell him she was a virgin to make him understand why she couldn't go on, but had she not let him in to begin with, none of this would've happened.

Ana readied herself for bed and for the first time in her life, she dreaded the following day on the job site.

Eight

Ana was surprised at the end of the next day when Zach hadn't stopped by. She never took him for a coward. Then again, she was relieved she didn't have to face the man who'd turned her world completely inside out with arousing caresses and captivating kisses.

She left the site later than expected because she'd lost track of time as she'd completed the payroll. She refused to admit she didn't want to go back to her condo where memories would smack her in the face as soon as she walked through the door.

But, as she slid the key card into the slot, she braced herself. It was just a room, just an incident. Zach had probably already wiped those moments from his mind.

Her cell vibrated and chirped against her hip as she entered the room. How ironic, she thought, looking at the caller ID, that Zach would call at the precise time she stood in the place where he'd broken through her line of defense.

"Hello."

"Sorry I didn't make it by the site today."

Ana leaned back against the closed door and tried to stop the chills from racing all over her body at the sound of Zach's low, sexy tone.

"That's okay," she said honestly. "What's up?"

"I've got this seating chart and it's driving me nuts. I know you've worked all day, but I need you."

He needed her. No matter what way he meant those words, she couldn't deny she loved hearing them.

"I'm fine." She walked farther into the room and began undressing. "Want me to meet you somewhere?"

"I'll pick you up. Can you be ready in thirty minutes?"

Considering she'd spent most of the day in her office with the cool air-conditioning, she didn't need a shower to rid herself of the grime and sweat she usually brought home at the end of her day.

Yeah, she just exuded sex appeal.

"Sure. See you in a bit."

She hung up before she could change her mind. Being close to Zach again was inevitable so she may as well get the first meeting after their make-out session over with.

After freshening up just a bit, she put on some mascara and lip gloss, and pulled her hair back in a loose knot at her nape. She hoped they weren't going anywhere fancy because she grabbed a pair of denim shorts and a pale blue tank, then slid her feet into white sparkly flip-flops. When she turned to look in the full-length mirror, she frowned. She looked like a teenager.

Zach knocked on her door before she could contemplate changing. That was fast.

When she opened the door, she forced a smile. She knew he'd act like last night hadn't been a life-altering moment, and it probably hadn't been for him, unlike for her. Even so, she had to put up a good front so he didn't know just how affected she was by what had happened.

"I'm ready," she told him, grabbing her purse from the small stand near the door. "I hope we're eating. I'm starving."

He smiled. "You like to eat, don't you?" he asked in a playful manner.

"What's not to like?" She closed the door and pocketed her key card. "I'd love a big steak or pizza."

Zach laughed, reaching to push the button on the elevator directly across from her door. "I've never dated a woman who didn't order a salad and then pick at it."

Her heart fluttered. She jerked to see him staring intently down at her. "Are we dating?"

"What do you say?"

Ana smiled, stepped into the elevator. "I say you're dating the wrong women if they're worried about keeping their figures the same as when they were teenagers."

Zach laughed, followed her in and punched the lobby button. "You're dodging me, Anastasia."

"You're the one who didn't show up today at the site."

Oops. She hadn't meant to sound like she'd been keeping time and waiting for him to show.

In a second, without warning, Zach turned, backed her against the back of the elevator and caged her in between his thick, muscular arms.

"You missed me."

It wasn't a question, but Ana shook her head anyway. "No, I just got used to you dropping by at least once a day."

His dark, seducing eyes sparkled. "Would you feel better if I told you I'd rather have been with you than in my office?"

"I'd feel better if you gave me some breathing room."

Zach placed a kiss on her lips and eased back just as the doors opened to the lobby. "For now."

Ana let out a pent-up breath as she followed Zach out the doors. She squinted against the sun, not seeing his Bugatti or Camaro.

"Over here," he motioned and walked toward his Harley.

She stood rooted in place. Of course he'd have a big, Alpha-style Harley with a matte black finish and just enough chrome to be flashy. "You're kidding," she said, glaring.

He pulled his sunglasses from his T-shirt pocket and slid them on. "What?"

"I'm not getting on that."

He swung his long leg over the seat, grabbed the spare helmet and held it out to her. Before she could tell him he was out of his mind, his cell phone rang. He grabbed it from his pocket.

"Hello."

She moved closer as he listened, grew concerned when he snapped toward her and asked the caller what happened.

"She's with me," he said into the phone. "We'll be right there."

"What's wrong?" she asked as he slid the phone back into his pocket.

He grabbed her hand and gave her the helmet, then tried to get her to get on the bike behind him. "Someone broke into your office at the site."

"I'll take my car," she demanded. "Stop tugging me."

"We'll go together."

She gave up arguing as fear and confusion took over. "Who called? Was there much damage?" She plopped the helmet over her head.

"That was Victor," Zach said. "He's getting ready to leave town for a few weeks and wanted to see how everything was going before he left. He swung by the property and noticed all the busted glass around your office. The windows are all shattered. He called the cops."

Zach reached around, adjusted the strap on her helmet. "Here."

Ana took a step back, holding up her hands. "You're

kidding me with this motorcycle, right? Why don't you drive a truck or something?"

"Because I live where the sun shines year-round and I like the freedom. Are we going to stand here and discuss my means of transportation or are you going to get on?"

She got on behind him and Zach started the bike.

He glanced over his shoulder and grinned. "You've never done this before, have you?"

Ana shook her head and put her arms around his waist. Thank God she'd chosen to wear shorts.

"You'll have to hold on tighter than that, Anastasia."

"Don't you wish," she yelled over the noise, but then he took off and she had no choice.

Ana didn't squeal like she wanted to, but she did shut her eyes as Zach flew through downtown Miami. The warm evening wind whipped the hair that stuck out from beneath the helmet. Slowly, lifting one lid at a time, she checked out the surroundings as they flew by.

If she weren't so worried about falling onto the pavement or the fact that some vandal had trashed her office, Ana would relish having her arms wrapped around one extremely muscular man. Beneath her palms and linked fingers lay his hard, chiseled abs under a thin black T-shirt. Wrapped by her legs, his lean thighs felt strong and sinewy. Ana couldn't help but lean forward, just a bit, and breathe in Zach's spicy, masculine scent. Between the vibration beneath her and the strong man against her, Ana was having some serious thoughts about taking Zach up on his offer and just giving in to the inevitable.

In no time they were pulling onto the site. A squad car was parked next to a sleek, black sports car. Ana's instincts went on alert as she took in the equipment, the area partitioned off for the resort. From an initial glance, everything seemed in order, except of course for the glass around her office trailer.

Zach pulled to a stop and killed the engine. "You can let go."

"Oh."

Ana jerked her hands away from his warm body, almost sorry the ride had come to an end. Even though she was a little shaky about the new, exhilarating experience, she could totally understand why Zach loved the bike so much. And the freedom he talked about, well, that just went hand in hand with Zach's lifestyle.

She climbed off the bike, waited for Zach to get off then handed him the helmet. "Let's go see what the damage is."

He walked beside her step for step. His silence spoke volumes. Zach, Mr. Always a Good Time, was quiet because he was just as scared and nervous as she—at least she assumed so. They couldn't afford disasters or setbacks on this job or any other. Earlier in the week she'd been worried about the potential threat of a tropical storm, one that had thankfully turned out to sea. But vandalism was something else again. True, it occurred occasionally on a job site, but with the rains and the firing of an employee, she hadn't had time to think about the off-hours when the site was left unattended. Besides, she'd only been gone about an hour tonight.

The epiphany hit her hard.

Ana stopped, grabbed Zach's arm to stop him as well. "What if this was revenge?"

Zach looked into her eyes. "We're thinking on the same page. You need to tell the officer exactly what Nate said about my sister, what you said when you fired him and an address where he can be found."

Ana nodded, glancing up as the officer and Victor Lawson came from inside the trailer. The grim look on Victor's face didn't help diminish her nerves.

"Much damage inside?" Zach asked.

"It's been trashed," the officer explained. "I assume you're the foreman?"

"No," Ana corrected, drawing the officer's attention to her. "I am. I'm Ana Clark and this is Zach Marcum, the architect."

The officer jotted down some notes on his pad. "You'll have to go in and see if anything was taken."

Ana turned toward Victor. "I can't tell you how sorry I am. I will hire a security guard to watch over the site in the off-hours."

Victor's generous smile eased her concern somewhat. "I assure you, this is not the first time a project of mine has been tampered with and I've already called a security team. They will be here tomorrow."

"I'll stay here tonight," Zach offered.

Ana jerked her head around. "I will. This is my site."

"Great, I'd love the company," he said with a wink.

Ana narrowed her eyes at him. If he was purposely trying to annoy her, well, mission accomplished. She wasn't going to get into an argument here and now with an audience.

She turned to her shattered office. "I'm going to check the trailer."

"Don't touch too much," the officer said. "It's still a crime scene and the crime scene unit should be here anytime to check for fingerprints."

She moved around the three men and climbed the rickety steps. They'd left the door open and Ana scanned the wreckage from the doorway. Files were flung everywhere, desk drawers had been dumped all over the floor. Luckily there wasn't too much paperwork and she knew Zach had all the duplicates in his office, but the fact that some jerk had torn apart her space made her furious.

"Could've been worse."

Zach's warm breath and voice were right behind her. She glanced over her shoulder, thankful he stood so close. His sunglasses were perched on top of his windblown hair, his dark eyes taking in the mess.

Why was her body reacting to this man? Why couldn't she have a barrier around her hormones that prevented the penetration of sex appeal brought on by cocky, overbearing men?

She'd always heard that women were attracted to men with qualities like their fathers'…. Obviously the case with Zach.

He flaunted himself, his money, his relationships, and all for the sake of a good time. He didn't care what people thought of him but, ironically, people still flocked to him.

The man thought he could have everything and no matter how attracted she was on a physical level, her emotions wouldn't go any deeper.

Still, she had to admit he was continually surprising her. He stepped closer and placed a comforting hand on her shoulder. His gentleness shocked her. She remembered last night when they were on the verge of intimacy in her condo. He couldn't have been any gentler with her. Not even as she'd dropped her bombshell when it was almost too late.

Nine

"I'll bring a couple of air mattresses." Zach urged her forward and stepped into the cluttered space. "You can bring the coffee."

Ana rolled her eyes. "We're not having a slumber party, Zach, and you're not staying."

The CSU had left powdery residue all over and she wanted to clean up and have a moment to herself without his sexy gaze on her. She was beyond pissed that someone had messed with her site.

Zach propped his hands on his narrow hips. "Oh, I'm staying. You're more than welcome to join me, but you won't be here alone."

Mimicking his stance, she rested her hands on her hips as well, more than eager to go toe-to-toe with him. "Look, this won't be the first, or the last, time I sleep in my on-site office. I don't need a babysitter. I'm sure whoever did this was just pulling a prank. We can't be sure it was Nate and even if it was, he probably feels better about getting out his frustrations. I'll bet this is the last we'll see of him."

A muscle in Zach's jaw clenched as he stepped closer. "I'm not chancing your safety. Besides, this will give us time to go over my sister's to-do list."

Ana wanted to argue, but Zach was genuinely concerned; she could tell by the low, slow voice. He wasn't joking anymore which meant he was still worried. Maybe she shouldn't be so quick to brush off the incident.

"If you stay—"

"I'm staying," he interrupted.

"Fine. You will keep your hands and all other body parts to yourself. Are we clear, Don Juan?"

The corner of Zach's mouth kicked up. "Yes, ma'am."

She found herself biting the inside of her cheek to keep from smiling back at him. Damn, the man had a contagious smile.

Her cell rang, pulling her from the moment. She pulled the phone from her bag.

"Hello."

"Oh, thank God. I've called twice this evening, Anastasia." Her mother's worried, frantic tone had Ana's back stiffening, her heart speeding up. "I'm sorry to bother you, honey. Are you terribly busy?"

"Not too busy for you. What's wrong?" She turned so she wouldn't have to look at Zach's questioning gaze.

"I don't know how to say this." Her mother's voice cracked. "Your father and I are filing for divorce."

Heart in her throat, Ana eased back against her desk, saw Zach step beside her out of her peripheral vision. "What?"

"I'm so sorry to have to tell you over the phone," her mother cried. "I just wanted to tell you before you heard it anywhere else. I finally left him."

Ana didn't know whether to congratulate her or offer her sympathies. "Mom, where are you now?"

"I'm at the last property your father hasn't gambled away... the beach house in Georgia."

"Do you need me to come to you?" Ana asked, her heart breaking for her mother.

"Oh, no, dear. I know how important this job is for you. I'll be just fine."

Would she? After thirty years of marriage, her husband's numerous affairs and being all alone in the end, how could anyone sound so positive? Pride for her mother overtook Ana. The amount of strength this woman exuded was remarkable. And the fact that Lorraine Clark hadn't committed an unspeakable, illegal action against the man Ana loosely termed "father" was a feat in itself.

"Call me anytime, Mom. I mean it. As soon as I'm done with this project, I'll take some time off and we'll go somewhere to relax."

Her mother let loose a watery laugh. "I'd really like that, Ana. I love you."

"Love you," Ana said, trying to choke back tears. "I'll call you tomorrow."

Ana disconnected the call, straightened and turned her back once again to Zach.

"I'll just go outside and speak with Victor and the officer," he told her, obviously taking the hint she needed some alone time. "They should be about finished here."

Well, that was one good thing that came from him knowing women so well. He was in tune with their feelings.

Ana swiped at a tear that had escaped. She didn't want to cry about this. Hadn't her father caused enough anguish over the years? He never seemed to care whom he hurt, so long as he got what he wanted. Women, money, the thrill of the next bet. He always took from everyone, never giving even a piece of himself in return.

And her mother had finally had enough. After thirty years.

Did happily-ever-after even exist anymore? She wished she could be there for her mother right now, but their reunion would have to wait.

"They're gone."

Ana jerked around to see Zach closing the office door. "Oh, um, didn't they need to talk to me some more?"

"I told them you had an emergency call and you'd come down to the station in the morning to let them know if anything was taken and to file an official report."

Ana tugged her rubber band from her hair, smoothed the tangled curls back as best she could and looped it back into a low bun. "Thanks. Guess I'd better start cleaning up."

Zach crossed the tiny space, stepping over files and papers, and came to stand within inches of her. "Care to tell me what but that tear track on your cheek?"

"Not right now."

He studied her face. "We're going to be bunk mates all night. I'm here when you're ready to talk."

Torn, Ana stood still as Zach began to pick up the papers and put them in stacks on her desk. Not only had he dropped the subject, he'd genuinely been concerned and offered her a listening ear later. Just like last night when her emotions and feelings were all over the place, he'd known when to give her space and say just the right words.

Okay, so maybe some good qualities did come from him being a playboy. Ana wasn't sure. But she did know one thing. She had to be on her guard where this man was concerned because if she wasn't careful, he'd cause more damage to her life than any vandalism or divorce ever could.

She was on a slippery slope and losing her grip fast falling for Zach Marcum. Each day she slid just a bit more. Unfortunately he wasn't on the slope following her down.

Cole and Tamera had brought fast food, an air mattress, pillows and a couple of lightweight blankets. After Zach assured his twin and Tam that he and Ana would be fine sleeping in the on-site office, they finally walked out.

But not before Cole motioned for Zach to join him outside.

"Could I have a word with you?" Cole asked.

"Be right back," Zach told Ana.

Cole sent Tamera on to the car and stood at the bottom of the wrought-iron steps waiting for his fiancée to be out of earshot.

"Don't screw this up."

Zach rested one black boot on the top step, the other on the bottom step. "I'm not screwing anything up."

"I know you," Cole stated. "I also know Ana isn't your type but the two of you are shooting off some pretty strong sparks. I was serious when I told you you couldn't get her because she wasn't your type and she wouldn't be interested."

Zach shrugged. "I never take you seriously. Was there anything else?"

"She's not here for your enjoyment, Zach," Cole warned, lowering his tone. "I haven't spent much time around her, but there's a sense of innocence about her. She's a professional. Make sure you stay that way as well."

Anger bubbled to the surface. Between the break-in, Ana's upsetting phone call that he still ached to know about and Cole's fatherly warning, Zach was ready to explode.

"If you're finished letting me know how to live the next year of my personal and professional life, your fiancée is waiting."

Without another word, he turned and went back into the cool office where Ana was setting up the air mattress in the middle of the floor. Every window, save for the one with the small air-conditioning unit, had been busted. They'd boarded them up in order to keep in the cool air.

On her knees, pulling the air pump from the suction of the

mattress, Ana glanced up as he came back through. "Home sweet home." She smiled.

Even though she tried to keep her tone light, Zach caught the question underlying her statement. When her eyes darted to the bare bed, the stack of pillows and sheets on the desktop and back to him, he knew she was worried. Cole had only brought one mattress.

"Ana, you don't have to stay here." He closed the door behind him, not moving much farther into the tiny office. There was no reason to make her any more jittery. "I'll be just fine. In all honesty, I'm sure whoever did this won't be back tonight, if ever. I can call Cole back and have him give you a lift home."

Shaking her head, Ana came to her feet. "Don't be absurd. I'm not going anywhere. I meant that the first and second time I said it."

"You're nervous."

"Yes."

He smiled at her quick, honest answer. "Don't be. I also didn't lie when I said nothing would happen until you're ready. I would never push you, Ana."

"I'm not concerned about you, Zach." She crossed her arms over her abdomen. "I'm scared of myself."

"Excuse me?"

She sighed, moving around the mattress to lean against the small desk that had been shoved into the corner. Her long, lean legs extended out in front of her. Zach held his place, waiting for her to continue.

"I don't recognize myself lately," she said, staring down at her jeweled flip-flops. "You make me want things I've never wanted before. Make me have thoughts about something other than work and my family. I've never thought about…"

"Yourself?" he asked, earning him a slight nod. "You're too busy working or taking calls from your parents or helping people who need you. You can't say no to anyone, so therefore your own needs are put on hold."

Ana brought her gaze back up to his. "You're not telling me anything I don't know, but I just don't know how to let go."

Easing closer, Zach shrugged. "I can't believe this is coming from my mouth, but take it slow. I don't want you to regret being with me. And since we're here all night, and my first choice of activities isn't an option, we'll work on the seating chart for the shower."

Ana's eyes studied him for a moment. And now that he'd moved closer, he could see just how hard her pulse was pounding. Out of nerves? Or arousal?

"I never know what you'll do or say next," she murmured. "You're not who I thought you were."

That made two of them. He had no idea he'd ever want to put his social life on hold to wait for a woman who may or may not ever be ready to sleep with him. And if/when she did decide, what the hell then? He had nice words to give her about waiting and being patient, but when the time came, could he really give her everything she needed? Would he be attentive enough, gentle enough?

"Let me go get the list of names," he told her, once again heading back outside, needing some distance. "I'm going to move my bike closer to the office, too."

He walked out into the sun setting over the ocean to retrieve the list from the saddlebags on his Screamin' Eagle and couldn't help but think of how far they still had to go on this property.

Normally when a project started, Zach was in a hurry to see it completed. Not this time, though. Because when this resort was done, Ana would move on to another town, another site. Another man?

Zach kick-started his Harley to life and gritted his teeth.

No, he was in no hurry to see this project come to a close, but he wouldn't dwell on the inevitable. Right now, he was working on his master plan of seduction.

Ten

Nerves slammed around in Ana's body as she waited for Zach to come back. Was this fate's way of smacking her in the face by giving her the opportunity with a man she knew could show her everything she needed to know and more about intimacy?

Yes, Zach's willingness to be her teacher wasn't her concern. The fact that she knew without a doubt that her heart would get battered in the process was more bothersome.

Ana slipped out of her flip-flops and took the pile of sheets to make up their bed.

Their bed.

There was no way that she could sleep with Zach on this mattress. No. Way. She'd never shared a bed with anyone, much less a man.

This was a bad, bad idea. So what if Cole only had one mattress in his attic? Why didn't he just go buy another one? Probably because Zach told him not to.

Ana snapped the fitted sheet from the folded pile and

wrestled the elastic corners over the air mattress, all the while cursing the blasted person or persons who were responsible for the break-in. Not only did they make a total mess of her meager work space, but so did the cops, and now she was forced to be with Zach and his sexy smile, powerful words and arousing touches.

Just as she sent the top sheet sailing into the air to let it fall carelessly over the bed, Zach stepped back in with folded papers in hand and an expression she couldn't quite read.

"What's wrong?" she asked.

He shook his head, laid the papers on her desk. "Nothing— other than the fact that your office got trashed, I'm stuck with this guest list while my sister is out of town and this is not how I wanted to spend an evening alone with you."

Ana couldn't help but laugh. "Careful. Your bottom lip is starting to pucker. Pouting won't change a thing."

"You're right, but you asked." He glanced down to the bed in the middle of the floor, then back up to her. "You know there's no way we can sleep on that."

Yeah, she knew. She was just surprised he thought so.

"I'll take this blanket and sleep on the floor by the door," he told her, grabbing the thin cotton blanket from her desk chair.

"I'm not tired." Ana didn't want to get into sleeping arrangements right now. Her nerves were already a jumbled mess. "Let's look at the guest list and see how many people you all should expect so we can get some numbers to your caterer."

Zach spread the blanket out on the hard floor and came back over to where Ana had the papers spread across her desk. His cologne wasn't overpowering, but it was strong and dominating, just the same. Much like the man.

She knew her office was small, even more so every time he'd been in here, but now that she knew they were going to be here for hours, through the hot, hopefully silent night, the space really seemed to close in around her.

Ana stared down at the papers, resting her hands on the edge of her desk, right alongside of Zach's. Yeah, there wasn't a word on there that she could focus on. How could she when all she could think about was whether she should take this opportunity and run with it?

But at the same time, just because the opportunity was there, did that mean she had to act on it?

"...and since we're going with the ice cream social and mingling motif, seating won't be an issue so we won't have to worry about dealing with exes and people who would rather not be seated next to their in-laws."

Ana dragged her mutinous mind back to the issue at hand. Forcing herself to listen to Zach, she nodded. Zach seemed to have it all sorted out. Obviously he wasn't having an issue at all.

"The names printed in red are the ones who are coming." He pointed to another set of names. "These in green haven't sent their RSVP back in yet."

Ana cleared her throat. If he could manage this crackling tension, then so could she. "How many of these are children?"

Zach ran a long, tanned finger down the last page. "She has here approximately seventeen."

"Okay, so we'll need two dozen cupcakes at least," Ana told him, grabbing a pen from her desktop and jotting down notes on the list. "I'd say more like three dozen, though. I assume Kayla will take care of calling the caterer?"

Zach nodded. "She should be back tomorrow, so yes, she'll do that."

Ana picked up a small notepad from her desk and moved to the mattress. She sank down, crossing her legs and began to jot more notes down, trying desperately to get into the role of wedding shower coordinator and keep her distance from Mr. Tall, Dark and Yummy.

No such luck. He followed her, removed his black boots and sat next to her on the bed. Because he outweighed her by a good fifty pounds, she had to catch herself from tumbling against him.

"What are you writing now?" he asked, leaning closer to get a look.

"Just some of my thoughts for Kayla. I—"

Zach placed a hand over her hand on the pen. "You're shaking."

Ana kept her eyes diverted to the paper and forbid herself from looking up into a set of chocolate eyes she just knew were watching her every move.

But she wasn't about to act like the unknowing, naive woman who didn't know what he was referring to. "I tend to shake when I'm nervous."

"Do I make you nervous, Anastasia?"

She risked a glance over at him—so much for her forbidding herself. "Only when you're with me," she said with a slight smile.

His warm fingers stayed wrapped around her hand, but his other hand came up to the base of her throat. "Your pulse is always going so fast. Are you scared?"

"I'd be a fool not to be scared." She closed her eyes, allowing his sensual touch to take over. "You promised not to push me."

"You don't look like you're being pushed into anything." She heard the smile in his voice. "You appear to be enjoying my persuasion."

Those wandering fingers came up around her jawline, slid over her slightly parted lips and stroked them. "You like my touch, don't you?"

"Yes," she whispered.

The pen slid from her hand, rolled off her lap. The notebook slid onto the sheet as well.

"Why don't you just let your body take over?" he whispered, moving in closer. "I know you have so much passion."

Oh, how she wanted to let him take complete control over this situation. But she couldn't. If she let him in, even the slightest bit, she feared he'd leave her wanting more of something he couldn't give.

She came to her feet, nearly tripping backward as she stumbled off the mattress. "This isn't happening. It can't."

Zach's gaze started at her bare feet, traveled up her legs and body before locking onto her eyes. "It will happen, Ana. You want this just as much as I do and you won't deprive yourself for long. One of these times when we're alone, you'll lose control. And I'll be there ready and willing."

Shivers slid up Ana's spine at the matter-of-fact tone. "Are you always this sure of yourself?"

His grin was menacing, threatening. Arousing. "Always."

She stepped back once again when he came to his feet and held out his hand. "Come on," he told her. "I have an idea."

Keeping her hands to herself, she eyed him. "What?"

"Just come on." He pulled his boots back on, tossed her flip-flips her way and grabbed his keys. "I'm going to be your first one way or another."

"You can't be serious," Ana exclaimed once they stepped outside her office into the stifling Miami heat. Even though it was nearly midnight, the air was thick and Zach's idea was preposterous.

He smiled, crossed his arms over his wide chest and shook his head. "This is the perfect spot for you to learn how to ride."

Ana stared at the big, black motorcycle like it would bite her. "There's no way I'm getting on that and driving it."

"Why not? I had a first time, too."

She laughed. "I don't want to hear about your firsts and I don't want to learn."

He leaned down next to her ear and whispered, "We can always go back inside."

Ana swallowed. "Give me a helmet."

"No need." He eased back and handed the key to her. "We're just going to be around here and you won't be going fast. Besides, there are no rules on private property."

Still, fear of the unknown territory speared through her. "Zach, this is silly. What if I tear up your bike?"

He shrugged, took her hand and placed it on the handlebar. "You won't tear it up and if you do, it's a piece of metal. It can be fixed and I have others."

The warm metal beneath her palm did nothing to soothe her nerves. "Is there anything I should know before I mount up?"

Zach let out a deep-from-the-belly laugh, smacking a kiss right on her cheek before he came around the other side of the bike. "Mount up? No, there's not much you need to know. I can stand here and tell you that this is a Harley-Davidson Screamin' Eagle specially made when I ordered it. I could go through the impressive engine I had put into it, along with all the accessories, but I won't bore you.

"Right now all you need to know is how to sit on it before you start it. Get used to holding all that power between your legs."

She quirked a brow. "You're seriously not going to start with those double entendres, are you?"

Zach shrugged. "If that's the only way to ease you into everything. Now sit."

"Don't I need pants and boots or something?"

He glanced to her bare legs and flip-flops. "Nah. The engine won't get hot in the little bit of time you'll be riding. That is if you can get it started and can steady it."

Ana rolled her eyes. "Like I said. How hard is it to sit with this thing between your legs?"

When Zach merely smiled, those stark white teeth shining bright compared to his tanned skin and dark rugged stubble on his jaw, Ana knew she was in over her head.

And not just with the Harley.

Keeping her hand firm on the handle, she tossed her leg over the seat and grabbed hold of the other handle. "Okay, now what?"

He stood in front of the bike, arms crossed over his impressive chest, the hint of a tattoo on his bicep peeking from beneath his black T-shirt. Well, that answered one question. One down, how many hidden tattoos to go?

With the moon behind the clouds, this sexy, irresistible man before her looked like the polar opposite of a millionaire CEO type…. He looked like the devil wrapped in a nice, enticing package.

"Try to balance the bike between your legs. Put your weight on your feet and ease the bike so it's up and not leaning on the stand."

Her hands gripped the bars as she shifted her weight, and the bike. "Oh, no…"

He was right beside her, curling his big, strong hands around hers, shoving his rock-solid body against her side to prevent her from tilting.

"Good grief." Ana's breath came in fast pants, not just because of the near fall on this huge bike. "I had no idea it would feel that heavy. It didn't seem like that when I sat behind you."

She glanced up to see him mere inches from her face, his heavy-lidded eyes aimed right on her parted lips. "That's because I do all the work," he told her in a raspy tone.

"We're not talking motorcycles anymore, are we?"

He smiled, leaned in even closer, his lips barely a whisper

away from hers. "I was referring to everything in my life. But I like where your mind keeps wandering."

And then he didn't let her mind wander anymore. His smooth, soft lips covered hers in the kiss she'd been dreaming about for hours, for days. And Ana didn't even have the briefest of moments where she wanted to fight him or pull back. She wanted his mouth on hers.

Their hands still remained on the handles, but his fingers had slid between hers, stroking. Her shoulder still rested against the hard wall of his chest.

With a gentle sweep of his tongue, he eased her lips apart, taking the kiss to an even deeper level of intimacy.

How could he be so controlling, so demanding, yet so gentle and passionate?

Just when she thought for sure he'd put his hands someplace else on her body, he tugged slightly on her bottom lip, drawing out the kiss even more before easing back.

Her eyes fluttered open as she ran her tongue across her lips, trying to hold on to his taste.

"What about the police cruiser that's been driving by?" she whispered. "We can't—"

"He already drove by and they're only coming by every hour." Zach's bright smile cut through the darkness, and her resolve. "Plenty of time."

Nerves now settled in good and deep in her stomach. "Zach, I—"

Now his hands did come up to frame her face as he crushed her mouth under his. All words, and thoughts, were completely lost. She had no idea what she'd been about to say. Maybe she was going to tell him she couldn't go any further than heated kisses, but more than likely she was going to beg him not to stop. At least he'd saved her from begging.

Her body ached for him. Her hands fell off the handlebars as she turned to the left and reached around with her right hand to grab fistfuls of his shirt.

Zach's talented lips trailed heated kisses from her lips down her jaw and neck to the scoop of her tank top. Something in Ana took over—instincts, hormones, pure lust—did it matter? She arched into him, silently begging him to keep doing everything he was doing that made her feel so amazing.

"I can't stop, Ana. I can't stop touching you." He kissed her harder, then pulled back. "I won't push you, but I have to at least touch you anywhere you're comfortable with."

He pushed one hand up her tank and she could only groan out a "yes" when that warm palm slid up her abdomen and over her lacy bra.

Chills raced, one after the other, all over her body.

"This is for you," he murmured against her skin as he traveled back up to her mouth.

"What?"

She had no idea what he meant, but he didn't stop assaulting her shoulders, neck and lips long enough to answer.

Taking both hands to the waistband of her shorts, he made quick work of the button and zipper.

Was this really happening? Was she ready? If not, she feared in about one more second it would be too late to say so.

"Zach…"

He eased on the bike behind her. "Shh. Lean against me, Ana."

Falling back against that hard-planed chest she'd give anything to see bare, Ana tried to relax. But Zach's hands opened her shorts and one of his hands slid in.

Her body stiffened, but Zach murmured soothing words into her ear as his other hand eased back up her shirt. Ana didn't know where to put her own hands, so she rested them on Zach's thighs and squeezed when his fingertips caressed her between her legs.

"Relax, Ana. This is all for you."

Her hips jerked as she tightened her hold on his thick,

muscular legs. Easing her legs open wider, Ana did as he told and let herself go.

Zach used both of his hands in ways she'd never dreamed possible. She didn't know if he was torturing her or pleasuring her. A fine line separated the two emotions.

Just when she thought she couldn't take another second of agony, her body tightened, convulsed. Pleasure like she'd never known shot through every corner of her body.

Whatever Zach whispered in her ear was lost in the hot Miami night. His stubbled jaw rasped against her cheek as her tremors slowly died down.

Embarrassment threatened to take over, but Zach, as usual, knew where her thoughts were headed.

"So responsive." He eased his hand from her shorts, placing it on the inner part of her thigh. "That was the sexiest moment of my life."

Ana closed her eyes, wishing she could believe his words, but knowing he probably did this all the time with women. Perhaps he'd even said those exact words.

Hey, get on my bike and I'll show you how to ride.

And she'd fallen for his line. But with the way her body tingled, she'd worry about her foolishness tomorrow. Right now she was too busy relishing the way her body still hummed.

Oh, she'd made out with men, but never had she even come close to climaxing. Nothing about Zach resembled any relationship she'd had in the past. And that was the scariest part of it all. She wasn't even in a relationship with him; he was her boss.

"I think I've had enough lessons." She tried to ease away, but his arms tightened around her.

"Don't be upset."

"With whom?" she asked. "You or me?"

"Me for showing you a new side to your own body and you for thinking you lost control." He straightened her clothes, even refastened her pants, and wrapped his arms around her waist. "Sometimes loss of control is a good thing, Ana. I will apologize if you think I lured you out here for that. I really had every intention of you learning to ride."

She pried his arms from her and not so gracefully removed herself from between his legs and off the bike. "Yes, well, neither type of riding will happen again. It can't. Yes, I'm attracted to you. Obviously. But we can't have a fling while we're working and then afterward just go our separate ways. I don't do flings, Zach. And that's all you do. Surely I'm not the only one who sees the problem."

She didn't wait to hear his reaction. With jittery legs and a rapid heart, Ana climbed the rickety stairs to her office. After kicking her flip-flops into the corner, she flopped down on the air mattress and jerked the sheet up over her heated body.

He was right. She didn't know if she was upset with herself for playing right into his hand or him for making her see just what she was missing.

Ana had a feeling she still didn't know what she was missing because for some reason, even though Zach had pleasured her, she still felt cheated by not seeing him or touching him in return.

Damn that man. He'd gotten around her wall of defense, but he wouldn't get around the one to her heart.

That wall was made of steel.

Eleven

When the sun rose, Zach was still fully awake. And aroused. He'd spent the last six hours cursing himself for pushing Ana into something she mentally wasn't prepared for and pushing himself to the brink of insanity.

He'd never, ever been so adamant, so demanding about pleasuring a woman and receiving nothing in return.

But the intensity with which he'd wanted to pleasure her overrode any physical ache he'd had. He'd wanted her to see just a glimpse of the passion they could share, the desires that were swirling around them. Dancing around the sexual attraction for weeks was damn near killing him.

Knowing he'd maybe ruined any chances of getting her into his bed hurt much more than his stiff back from leaning against the wall at the foot of her mattress all night. Yes, he'd watched her sleep, trying to figure out how the hell he could get her to understand there was nothing to be ashamed of, nothing to regret. And so much more to explore.

But he knew the moment those mesmerizing green eyes

opened, he'd see regret filling them and there wasn't a damn thing he could do about it.

Zach came to his feet, picked up his boots and stepped outside, careful not to wake Ana. He sat on the top step and shoved his feet into his shoes.

Workers would be arriving in an hour or so. Some construction companies didn't start so early, but Ana didn't cut her employees slack where hours were concerned. She wanted them early, prompt and ready to get to it. Which was a smart move considering the hellish Miami heat.

Another thing he admired about her.

Dammit, he was treading on shaky ground here. He didn't want to admire her. He wanted to get her into his bed and get her out of his system. Then once the project was completed and Victor Lawson was thrilled about his first U.S. resort, then Zach could walk away feeling satisfied and one more giant leap past Melanie.

A small four-door car pulled into the dusty lot, gravel crunching beneath the tires. Zach turned to the vehicle, wondering who on earth could be here this early.

A tall, slender man with dark hair stepped from the car. The sun glinted off his hair, making the red more prominent. There was something about him that seemed familiar, but Zach knew he'd never met the man before.

"Morning," the man said as he closed the car door and approached Zach. "Didn't expect anyone to be here this early, except my girl. She's always prompt."

His girl. This was Ana's father. Zach loathed him on the spot and wondered what the hell the man could want.

"You work for Anastasia?"

Zach crossed his arms over his chest, wishing he'd woken Ana so she could be prepared for this surprise guest. "Technically she works for me. I'm the architect, Zach Marcum."

He didn't extend his hand by way of most initial meetings.

Zach had no desire to shake hands with a man who'd obviously hurt Ana on a level he couldn't possibly understand.

The man placed his hands on his hips, eyes narrowed. "Where's Ana?"

Before Zach could respond, the office door opened. Ana stood on the top step, wiping her eyes. All that auburn hair draped her shoulders in curls, and her tank and shorts were wrinkled from an uncomfortable night's sleep.

She hadn't spotted her father yet and Zach figured her eyes were still adjusting to the bright morning light. She stretched her arms above her head, baring a pale shimmer of midriff between her tank and shorts. What he wouldn't give to scoop her into his arms and take her away where they could be alone.

But he knew the second she spotted them. Her eyes, which had been scanning the horizon, now froze. She shoved her hair from her face, swept it over her shoulders and tilted her chin.

"What are you doing here?" she asked, without moving from the top step.

Zach turned so he was in between the two. He took a step back, though, to let them talk, but he wasn't going far.

"Just wanted to stop by to see my girl."

Ana rolled her eyes, rested her hands on her hips, mimicking her father's motion. "You've seen me, but I'm sure you're not here to make sure I'm okay or that I'm happy. So, let's cut to the chase, how much this time? And what are you doing in Miami?"

Zach saw the man's eyes turn to slits. "Can we talk in private?"

Looking to Zach, Ana shook her head. "Zach's not leaving unless he wants to. If you want something just come out and say it? How much are you in debt for this time?"

"Don't talk to me that way, young lady." Her father took

a step forward, putting Zach on full alert. "I'm still your father."

"You've never been a father to me," Ana said in a tone Zach had never heard from her. Pure venom dripped from her voice. "I'm just glad Mom finally came to her senses and left you, though you left her little choice when you squandered away everything she's ever owned."

"Why am I not surprised she called you crying? Look, Anastasia—"

"No." Ana held up a hand and came down the steps and closed the gap between her and her father. "You're just upset she called and told me because you know that now you have no leverage for me to fund your habit."

Zach moved toward his motorcycle, which was only a couple feet from this family feud. From the debt Ana referred to, Zach assumed her father had a gambling issue. Something he'd have to investigate on his own time.

"I just need ten thousand and I'll leave you alone," her father pleaded in a softer tone. "That's a small amount for someone like you. You've always hoarded every single dime you made and you've been at this business for a long time. I know how much you work yourself, too, so don't act like you don't have any money. Besides, I've been in Miami for a few weeks. I figured this is where all the high rollers come to play. Might as well see what I can get."

"You're pathetic to think you rank with people who actually worked for their money and were responsible enough to invest or pay off debts. I won't give you ten cents." Ana pointed a finger at her father, her tone growing louder and stronger. "If you want to play with the big boys, then step up and be one. Now get out of here before I call the police and have you arrested for trespassing."

A moment of silence stretched, but the tension still crackled. Finally her father spoke. "I can't believe you'd do this to me."

"Had you, even once, pretended you gave a damn about me and Mom, I would give you anything you wanted." Ana's voice hitched, the commanding voice she'd had seconds ago vanished as her vulnerability crept to the surface. "Had you ever told me you loved me, shown me that I mattered to you, I'd never question you and hand over everything I have without question. You didn't only gamble our money and assets, you gambled with lives. Mom and I will never get over how you destroyed our family."

Ana cleared her throat and Zach knew she was on the verge of tears. He wanted to go to her, wrap his arms around her and comfort her. But he wasn't sure how, not sure what to say. This was brand-new territory for him.

He did know one thing, though. He wanted Ana's father gone five minutes ago. But Ana had to deal with this herself. He wasn't her boyfriend. Hell, he wasn't even technically her lover, so this family reunion was none of his business.

"But you've never given me even one second of your life," Ana continued, her voice now stronger than ever, but Zach saw her eyes shimmering in the sunlight. "So I won't give you anything of mine."

Her father stood still for a moment, the muscle ticking in his jaw. "Fine. I hope you can live with yourself knowing you turned me away. I'll be in Miami for another week or so to see what turns up if you change your mind. I didn't raise you to be selfish, Anastasia."

"No, you didn't raise me at all."

He stalked away, got into his rental car and drove off the site, leaving Ana and Zach staring after the dusty trail.

"I didn't mean to oversleep." Ana turned toward Zach, pulled a rubber band from her pocket and twisted her hair back and looped it through. "I need to get to my condo and change so I can be back here before my crew shows up. Can you give me a lift?"

He lifted a brow. "Are you really going to pretend you're fine when I know you're not?"

"You know nothing about me, Zach."

Treading on shaky ground, he pushed his limit with her even further. It wasn't the brightest move to make, but he'd always gone against the odds and taken risks. No way was he going to let her brush this off when she was so upset.

"That's not true." He stepped around his bike, shoving his hands in his pockets to show her he wasn't threatening or confrontational. "I know you're hurting, I know you're vulnerable and I know you're regretting last night and the last thing you needed to wake up to was your father making demands."

His eyes held hers, saw the tears gathered there. She shut her eyes and one lone teardrop trickled down her creamy skin. The silent emotional plea took hold of his heart and squeezed. Hard.

"My personal business isn't your concern," she told him, eyes still closed as if trying to gather her courage to open them. "Can you just give me a ride back to my condo?"

Because he'd been dying to touch her the whole time her father had been here, Zach stepped forward and with the pad of his thumb wiped the moisture from her cheek. Her eyes popped open, and she bit her bottom lip and stared into his eyes.

"There's no need to hide your emotions." Zach left his hand on her cheek, cupping her soft skin in his palm. "I know you don't want to lean on anyone, but I'm here if you want to talk."

Her eyes searched his face. Surely she'd open up, let out what she'd kept bottled inside her. But she stepped back, making his hand fall to his side.

"All I need from you is a ride."

She walked around him and mounted the bike like a pro. Damn, she had a spine of steel. How could he not find that attractive? And how could he possibly stop himself from wanting her on more than a physical level?

Ana changed and was back at the site before the first member of her crew showed. As long as she kept going, didn't take time to think about her father's visit, she'd get through the day.

Oh, who was she kidding? She was used to her father always dropping in unannounced, begging for money. She needed to concentrate on work and stay busy so she didn't think about the one and only sexual experience she'd ever had, thanks to Zach and his talented hands.

Even inexperienced as she was, she had a gut feeling that he'd set the bar so high no other man could reach it.

Great. Exactly what she did *not* need.

This was just one more reason she'd never gotten involved with a man, never let him touch her body in such an intimate way. How could she work when her mind was replaying over and over the events of last night? How could she ever be alone with him again and not immediately desire to see what else he could teach her?

Zach had been so giving, so…perfect. Yes, much as she hated to admit it, he'd done every single thing right.

So why was she so ticked?

She slammed the door to her office, stared at the mess of sheets on the mattress where she'd slept. Alone. She'd rolled over last night and peeked from beneath her lids to see where Zach had gone. She was surprised to see him propped against the wall watching her.

A ripple of nerves speared through her as she recalled how he'd looked with the sliver of light filtering through the cracks in the boards over the windows.

He cared for her. Whether he wanted to admit it or not, he cared. He couldn't have been so giving, so gentle with her last night and expect nothing in return if he didn't. He wouldn't have stood by her side when her father showed up, then offered a shoulder to lean on if he was only out to take her virginity.

And the mind-blowing thought that big, bad playboy Zach Marcum was growing feelings for her scared her to death. He wouldn't like it when he realized the path his emotions had taken him down.

Of course, she could be wrong and he treated all of his women this wonderfully. That would explain why he always had so many.

But she didn't think she was wrong and now she'd just have to wait and see how the rest of their time together played out.

God help her heart when he walked away.

Twelve

Ana was back in her condo, freshly showered and in her cami/boyshort pajama set getting ready to comb out her hair when a knock sounded on her door.

She laid the wide-toothed comb on the vanity in the bathroom and walked through her master bedroom and the living area to the door and peeked through the hole.

Zach. Of course.

Being around him all day had been fine, seeing as how her entire crew was milling about. But now he chose to come to her alone, a one-on-one meeting, when he knew she'd be more vulnerable. Fantastic.

She opened the door, just enough for him to see her, but blocked his entry.

"Can I come in?" he asked.

In the span of a second, all the reasons flashed through her mind as to why he shouldn't come in. Her state of dress, or lack thereof, the pictures she never wanted to share that she had sitting around in her bedroom. Which wouldn't be an issue if he stayed out.

Oh, yeah, and another reason he shouldn't come in was the fact that she knew he'd want to discuss what had transpired between them last night and the confrontation this morning with her father. She needed armor to deal with Zach and not just in the form of more clothing.

"Now's not a good time." Wasn't that the truth?

A corner of his sexy mouth tipped up in a grin. "If I waited for a good time, you'd never let me in."

Why lie? "Probably not."

"Please," he said, all signs of joking aside.

"I'm not really dressed for company," she explained.

"If I promise to control myself, will you let me in?"

She wondered if he was capable of controlling himself, at the same time that she felt a bit disappointed that he wasn't here to finish what they'd begun last night.

What a mix of chaos her emotions were. One minute she wanted him to take her to places she'd never been and the next she wanted him to stay away.

"Ana…"

She bit her lip and eased the door open to allow him to pass through.

When she turned to face him, his gaze raked over her bare legs, her bra-free chest and her wet hair. And she just knew her nipples were now puckered. Why did her body have to betray her when she was trying to stand her ground?

Because she wanted this man. After the performance last night, she honestly wanted to see what else he would do.

"Let me get a T-shirt," she said, bypassing him and walking into her bedroom.

Thankfully all of her personal pictures were kept beside her bed and on the dresser. She would just have to keep Zach in the living room.

She grabbed an oversize T-shirt from the top dresser drawer

and was just pulling it over her head when he stepped into her bedroom.

"I didn't mean to intrude." He took a seat in the wing chair next to the window. "But at the site today, we didn't have any privacy and if we had managed to steal a moment, it wouldn't have been without interruptions."

Ana crossed over to him, leaned a hip against the window-sill. "I'm sorry you had to witness that not-so-pleasant family reunion this morning. I'd appreciate it if you didn't tell anyone what you overheard. My father... He has a gambling problem."

"I assumed as much."

Zach eased back in the chair, watching her. With very few words and an intense stare she knew he was listening as if he wanted to know what was going through her mind.

No man had ever given her the kind of personal attention Zach did. God, she didn't want to be one of those clichés. The woman who never had affection from her father fell for the first guy who showed her attention.

But in Ana's heart she knew, even if she'd had a father of the year as a kid, she'd still be tangled up with Zach emotionally.

"I'm not proud of the fact I've always paid off his debts," she continued, turning her gaze out the window to the bright pink sky meeting the clear blue ocean. "I only did because I love my mother and she's been through a hellish marriage. But now that she's left, I don't care what happens to him."

Saying those words aloud was so much different than thinking them. Ana ran her hands through her tangled hair as all of her twenty-eight years of emotions bubbled to the surface. "That sounds so cruel," she whispered, looking down to Zach. "I can't help that I don't love him. He never gave me a chance to. He's my father, but he never loved me. The first time in my life he ever paid attention to me was when I started making money. He became interested in my business...or so I thought.

"I was foolish enough to believe he saw me as an adult and we could start having a good relationship. I should've known better."

Zach reached out, took her hands in his and squeezed. "There's nothing wrong with wanting to be loved by your parent, Ana. That's something that you shouldn't have to beg for or pay for. Ever."

Tears clogged her throat as her eyes began to burn. "You're right, but that didn't stop me from paying every time he came to me. In the back of my mind I always thought maybe this time he's proud of me. He knows how hard I've worked for the money and he's going to recognize my accomplishments."

Ana didn't know why she was telling him all of this, but once she started, she couldn't seem to stop herself.

"You know, when I was a kid, I always wanted a dog." She pulled her hands free from Zach's and paced the room. "I overheard my mother begging for him to let me get one, but he told her the last thing they needed was something else depending on him."

Ana took a seat on the bed, crossed her legs beneath her as memories flowed out into the open. "I didn't ask for one again because I heard my mother crying in the bathroom right after that. Even as young as I was, I knew she was the only parent who loved me, who actually cared."

"Why didn't she leave him a long time ago?" Zach asked.

Ana lifted a shoulder. "At first I think it was because she got pregnant right after they got married and she quit working for my grandfather to stay home. My grandfather, the one I would tag along with on his construction sites, was old-school. Once you're married, you stay married, no matter what. Then as I got older, I think Mom was afraid to start a life being single, jobless and trying to take care of me. Dad still worked for Grandpa, so maybe she was just scared what that relationship would do. I honestly don't know."

"What about when you moved out?"

A question she'd asked herself many times. "I still think she was scared. She knew about his numerous affairs, his overexcessive spending habits, but she'd been living that nightmare for so long, I don't think she thought she could do better."

Zach came to his feet and Ana was sure he was coming to comfort her. Instead he moved to the nightstand and picked up a small frame.

She'd been so wrapped up in spilling her family secrets, she'd completely forgotten about the photos. But now Zach was holding one and no matter how much she wished she'd never let him step foot in her bedroom, she knew he'd taken an even bigger step into her heart.

Zach studied the picture of a young, even-more-innocent Ana and a lady who undoubtedly had to be her mother. Both were smiling for the camera, but their eyes were empty.

"You certainly take your beauty from your mother," he told her, trying to get her to think of something more positive. "How old are you here?"

Ana barely shot a glance at the picture he held. "Seven."

Gently he sat the picture back down as his eyes traveled over the others. There was another one of Ana and her mother. This time Ana was grown and the two were smiling, arm in arm sitting on the beach.

But it was the picture of Ana as a young child that captured his attention.

"This your grandfather?" he asked, pointing to the aged photo.

Ana turned and smiled at the picture as if she were looking at the actual man in the photo. "Yeah. He was the best."

Zach smiled at the toddler sitting on a bulldozer, with

red ringlets poking beneath a scratched-up hard hat. Her grandfather stood beside the machine, securing little Ana with one large tanned hand on her dimpled knees.

"He taught me everything I know," she told him. "I've never felt more alone than when he passed. It was hard for me to keep working, knowing I couldn't run to him for advice. My mother took his death the hardest, though. She truly was alone because my father was never around and I was off hopping from site to site."

Ready to make the next paycheck to send to her father to keep his habit going and keep a roof over her mother's head. Zach knew what she was thinking, but he wasn't going to intervene on this shaky ground.

"Nothing you can do about it now," he told her, trying to get that sad look from her eyes even if he had to make her angry at him. Anger he could deal with. Remorse and sadness, not so much. "Don't beat yourself up on someone else's mistakes."

She jerked her chin up, her eyes to him. "I'm not beating myself up. But I do get upset when I think of all my mother has gone through because my father couldn't control himself… in any way."

"She's a grown woman, responsible for her own actions, Ana." Zach eased down onto the bed beside her. "You're not helping anyone, especially yourself, by being depressed about this. You held your ground with your father today and he'll either straighten up or he'll pay the consequences. Either way, it's out of your hands."

She stared at him for a moment before coming to her feet and crossing to the window. With her back turned Zach couldn't help but allow his gaze to rake over all that delicate skin and the skimpy shorts that fit perfectly over her bottom.

Ironic that he'd never wanted anyone more than Anastasia. Yet here they were in her bedroom with the orange glow from the setting sun creating the perfect ambiance, and her wearing next to nothing, and they were only talking.

Yeah, this had never happened to him before. He'd come here to have another intimate encounter to get her to trust him a bit more. He had no idea he'd get in on an emotional battle she was waging with herself.

Personal issues were not things he ever allowed himself to get involved in with a woman. Families were messy, complicated—two things he didn't need when seducing a woman. He liked simple and straightforward.

"I'm sorry," she said in a soft voice, still keeping her back to him. "I didn't mean to just have an emotional dump. But with Dad's visit today, I'm just not the best company."

"Then let's talk about last night."

Zach watched her back stiffen, her body freeze as if she was holding her breath.

"What's to discuss?" she asked. "It happened, it won't again, so let's move on."

He came to his feet, slowly closing the distance between them. "When you talk fast like that, I know you're nervous which makes me believe you don't really mean what you just said."

She glanced over her shoulder, her eyes finding his. "You don't have to remind me again about this attraction, and yes, last night proves it. But we're different, Zach. I do require some commitment and even if I didn't, I can't split my time between the largest project I've ever taken on and something so personal and intimate all at once."

"That's why I'm perfect for you." He placed his hands on her slender shoulders and turned her to face him. "I'm here for you on both fronts. Ana, I'm persistent, you know that. Why fight what we both want? We'll sleep together by the end of the project anyway. Prolonging the inevitable won't change the outcome."

Her creamy cheeks reddened. "I don't know why I find

myself wanting you. You're sexy, and you've always been right by me when I've needed you, but then you pull out this arrogance that I can't stand and remind me of all the reasons I don't want to like you."

Tugging on her gently until she fell against his chest, Zach looked down into her eyes. "I don't care if you like me, Anastasia. I care if you want me."

He crushed his lips to hers, not taking the time to be gentle, just demanding. He knew no other way.

She'd driven him crazy for weeks. He was hanging on by the proverbial thread.

Ana ran her hands through his hair, holding him in place, as if he were going to go anywhere. She groaned when he nipped at her lips and then dove back in for more.

Yeah, there was no way this urge to have her would just disappear if they ignored it. His desire for her grew each time he saw her, touched her.

Zach's hands roamed down her back to cup her backside through the long T-shirt and boyshorts. What he wouldn't give to rip off all their clothes and show her just how arrogant he was. He wasn't laid-back, certainly never had been in an intimate setting, but Ana needed someone in her life to be. And, dammit if he wouldn't be that man.

Much as it pained him, literally, Zach eased back, moving his hands back to her shoulders to steady her.

"You don't need this now," he told her, never hating himself more for having morals.

She blinked in confusion. "Yes, I think I do."

As if she'd taken her small hand and clutched his heart, Zach felt the pressure deep in his chest. "You *think*. That's not enough. When you know for certain, come find me."

Zach turned, walked out of the condo and to the elevator before the ramifications of what he'd just turned down hit him.

Ana offering herself with no promises of commitment or questions about tomorrow.

He'd never turned down a woman he was interested in. Ever.

Obviously in his attempt to sneak past her line of defense, she'd gotten by his without so much as a warning.

He'd wanted to get past the complications of Melanie trying to wedge her way back into his life. Well, his wish came true. Now he just had an even bigger complication in the form of a fiery redhead with a tool belt.

Thirteen

After four infuriating weeks, Ana was ready to choke Zach Marcum. It was either that or drag him into her office and make him finish what he'd started on his motorcycle a month ago. What had he called it? A Screamin' Eagle? What an appropriate place to have such a memorable sexual experience.

How dare he assume that just because she wanted him that she'd act on her feelings? Granted, had he not pulled back in her condo, she would've consented to anything and everything he wanted. She'd been a vulnerable, emotional basket case.

But he'd gone and shocked her by leaving. Ana had no doubt he'd shocked himself as well. The evil part of her hoped he'd suffered because of his gallant effort to make sure she was certain about taking the next step.

As she thought about him, Ana fingered the invitation for the wedding shower today. For some insane reason, Kayla had invited Ana to Tamera's bridal shower.

Silly, really. She barely knew Tamera, since she'd dealt with mostly Zach. But Kayla had been so thrilled with the whole ice cream social idea, she'd insisted on inviting Ana. How out of place would *that* feel? What on earth did she have in common with any of these socialites? She was a forewoman. She didn't get weekly manis and pedis, she didn't visit a salon on a regular basis to tame her curls and she certainly didn't have the pedigree she was sure the women at the party had.

She was just a simple girl from the Midwest who just so happened to catch the eyes of several architectural firms and built her career one beam at a time. There was nothing fancy, nothing special, and certainly nothing glamorous about her.

So why was she standing in front of the floor-length mirror in her bedroom running a hand down one of the last dresses in her closet? The knee-length purple strapless would be okay for a wedding shower. Wouldn't it?

Rolling her eyes at her preposterous way of thinking and for always second-guessing herself, Ana grabbed her gift and purse and set out for what was sure to be an interesting day.

When Ana stepped from the building, ready to ask the valet to fetch her a cab, a driver stepped from a sleek, black Jag and rounded the hood with a smile.

"Miss Clark?"

Smiling in return, Ana nodded. "Yes."

"Mr. Marcum sent me." He opened the rear door and gestured her in. "He told me you were attending a party and wanted to make sure you got there and back with no problem."

Stunned, Ana stood rooted in place for a moment, then stepped toward the car. "Zach sent you to take me?"

"Yes, ma'am."

Just another check on Zach's gentleman list. Seriously, if the man didn't want women falling head over heels, why on earth did he insist on doing such romantic gestures? She needed to put a stop to this and soon. But that was certainly not an issue she'd take up with the friendly driver.

"Thank you."

Refreshing air-conditioning welcomed her as she slid onto the cool leather seat. Zach was not making her life easy and she had a good feeling he knew it. He wanted her to come to him. Begging.

But she was already halfway in love with the frustrating man and if she gave him the last piece of her vulnerability, there would be no turning back. Which meant that when Zach moved on, and his type always moved on, she would have no one to blame for her broken heart but herself.

Today, however, would not be about her or her insecurities. Today she would make the most of being introduced to new people and celebrating the love two people found a second time around.

Ana admitted, only to herself of course, that she was excited to attend the shower. It wasn't that often she was able to mingle with women and dress like a lady all in one day. She would certainly take this moment and relish it.

Yes, she positively loved her job and all the amazing structures she'd been trusted with, but she was still a woman. And going out in public where she could show that side was always a plus and not something she often turned down.

Actually she needed this break. A break from the site, a break from the pressure, a break from her parents' impending divorce. But most of all a break from Zach.

He'd been at the site every day, but he'd never been anything but a complete professional. Some women may think he'd lost interest, but she knew better. She'd felt his stare numerous times, saw the muscle tick in his jaw as if he were grinding his teeth to keep from saying something. And he always drove the same motorcycle he'd had the night he'd given her the first "lesson."

No, he hadn't given up. If anything, he was just getting started, plotting his next course of seduction…or attack, depending on how she looked at it.

Ana nearly groaned as the car pulled onto Star Island. Because Kayla had wanted the shower to remain small, intimate, yet still extravagant, she'd chosen to have it at Cole and Tamera's house. Since the wedding was being held there, Kayla figured the shower would be perfect there as well.

The professional side of her was excited to see the home of one of the best architects in the world. Of course, she'd love to see Zach's house as well, but she figured asking him would certainly give the wrong impression.

Heaven's sake, she didn't even know what the *right* impression was anymore. She'd give anything if her emotions would settle down on this volley back and forth. But she was a realistic woman. She knew, as well as Zach did, that they would end up making love. At least, that's what it would be on her end.

Before she could process that stimulating thought any further, the Jag had come to a stop in a wide, circular driveway and the driver was opening her door.

"Ma'am," he said, extending his hand.

Ana clasped the elderly man's hand and smiled. "Thanks so much for the ride."

He tipped his head down like a true Southern gentleman. "My pleasure, miss. I'll be right here when you're ready to leave, too."

Ana shook her head. "Oh, no. That's not necessary. I can find a ride back."

"I'm just following orders, ma'am."

"But I could be here for a couple hours."

He nodded once again and headed back to the driver's door. "That will be just fine, Miss Clark."

The driver got into the car and pulled around the driveway to get out of the way of the entrance. Ana stood there for a second, amazed, humbled, confused.

Pulling her phone from her purse, she punched in Zach's cell. She waited in the shade of the oversize mansion because it felt like five hundred degrees in the sun and she wasn't ready to step inside yet. Not when she wanted privacy for her call.

"Hello."

Ana gripped the phone with one hand, settled the package under her arm with the other and turned her back on the car that had just pulled up. "Quit sending me mixed signals."

"Ana." She heard the smile in his lazy voice. "Did you make it to the shower?"

"You know I did," she snapped. "I'm sure your driver already told you that and that he's waiting for me to leave."

"Of course. He's a driver, Ana, that's what he does. What's wrong all of a sudden?"

She glanced over her shoulder as two middle-aged women stepped from the car, packages in hand. Lowering her voice, she replied, "Not all of a sudden. You haven't been anything but professional for weeks and today you send your driver to pick me up."

"Ana, I just thought you'd appreciate being able to leave when you wanted. You don't really know anyone, so if you became uncomfortable, I wanted you to have a way out."

Another piece of her heart melted at his concern for her, even though she knew in his mind it was simple, logical. Still, no one had ever taken this much care with her, this much effort to win her trust and affection.

She swallowed the lump in her throat. "You care for me."

A soft chuckle from the other end vibrated through her. "Of course I do."

"But you haven't touched me in weeks, haven't called or stopped by after hours. You've been all business." She let out a sigh, not quite comfortable with baring her heart. "I wasn't sure anymore."

She hated admitting that, but she'd always been honest in every aspect of her life and she wasn't going to stop now just because Zach had her all torn up.

"Is that what you want, Ana? For me to touch you? To stop by after hours when I know you'll be alone?"

Another car pulled up as shivers raced through Ana's body. "Yes. I do. But I think for our sanity and the sake of this project, we need to keep our personal distance."

"You're not a coward, Anastasia."

She never had been, but then, she'd never had her heart on the line, either.

"Thank you for the driver, Zach."

Snapping her phone, Ana slid it back into her purse, re-adjusted the package under her arm and stepped up the wide, travertine steps leading to the arched entryway.

Women in beautifully colored sundresses chatted, laughed and mingled. A couple of children ran through the foyer, followed quickly by a mother extending her quick apology as she chased the kids.

Ana smiled and walked toward the back of the house in the hopes of finding Kayla or Tamera and to see where to put the gift.

She didn't have to wait long. The two women, looking stunning as always, were embraced in a sisterly hug. A small tug at Ana's heart almost brought tears to her eyes. What would it be like to have a sister or a friend so close she felt like one?

Traveling down that path of thoughts would only get her into trouble. She'd come to terms years ago with being an only child, and she didn't stay in one place long enough to make any friends. And she certainly couldn't bring herself to get too attached to Zach's family. Being attached to the man was bad enough. She didn't want to have to cut any more ties than necessary when the resort was done and she moved her crew to the next location.

Shoulders back, chin high, Ana walked out onto the stone patio area like she belonged at this intimate social gathering.

"Ana," Kayla greeted with a wide grin. "I'm so glad you could make it."

Accepting the half hug from Zach's baby sister warmed her. "Thanks for inviting me. Where should I put this?" she asked, lifting the gift.

"I'll take that."

Kayla plucked the present from her and took it over to a table loaded with colorful boxes of all sizes and shapes and bags overflowing with tissue paper.

"Everything looks beautiful." Ana glanced around the lush tropical gardens that were obviously professionally maintained, then turned her attention to Tamera. "Congratulations."

The stunning blonde was literally beaming from ear to ear. "Everything is perfect. I understand I have you to thank for this creative idea. I absolutely love the relaxed atmosphere, and having desserts was brilliant. I seriously can't thank you enough for suggesting this."

Embarrassed, Ana merely shrugged. "It's really no big deal. Zach was in a bind, Kayla had business that took her away and I happened to be there. I just suggested what I would've liked."

Tamera studied her for a moment and Ana suddenly felt like she was under a microscope. She glanced around for Kayla, but saw her taking other guests' presents to the table.

"Zach's mentioned how efficient you are," Tamera said, still smiling. "I have to say, I've never seen him in such a good mood. And, come to think of it, I haven't seen him date in over two months. That's a dry spell for Zach."

Ana remained speechless. What could she say?

"Unless…" Tamera quirked a brow.

"No," Ana said, shaking her head. "No unless. We're working together, and yes, we've become friends, but that's all."

Tamera's smile dimmed down to a knowing grin. "I know how it is with the Marcum twins. Cole is just as potent as

Zach, but Cole always had that quieter, more subtle approach. Zach's is more full-force, knock-you-to-your-knees. But their effect is the same, so if you need to talk, I'm here."

Ana could only nod. Seriously, what could she say? That she'd already experienced that knock to her knees? That there was no way she could ever build up an immunity to Zach Marcum? That every time she was around him she second-guessed every personal decision she'd made about keeping her distance?

Yeah. She was much better off sticking with a simple nod and keeping her mouth shut.

"Ana." Kayla came up behind her and placed a hand on her arm. "The ice cream and toppings are through this set of double doors to the left. In the living area are all the cakes. And out here are all the finger-type desserts—cookies, cupcakes, fruit dipped in chocolate." She gestured at the tables all around her. "If you need something, don't hesitate to ask."

"I think I just gained ten pounds listening to the menu," Ana joked. "I'll walk around and see what appeals to me."

"Oh, I see one of my old clients," Tamera said. "Excuse me for just a moment."

Kayla ended up walking around with Ana, giving Ana the prime opportunity to quiz her about Zach. But Ana didn't. She was truly enjoying Kayla's company and couldn't bear to be sneaky and selfish just to gain an insight into Zach's interesting lifestyle.

But when she told Kayla about the driver Zach had sent and how the poor man was outside waiting on her, Kayla smiled and rolled her eyes and went and told the man he could leave. Since the order came from a Marcum, the driver obeyed once Kayla assured him she would take Ana home and take any of the backlash from Zach.

The shower was a huge success. Ana lost track of the time and didn't once think about Zach or how she could possibly keep her distance in a personal manner. For once, she truly felt at home, like she belonged.

She *oohed* and *ahhed* with the rest of the ladies over the gifts. Platinum candlesticks, picture frames, crystal vases, even an oil painting of the happy couple, provided by Kayla. At that gift, the entire room teared up, except for the few children who were still running their poor mothers in circles.

Ana wondered if she'd ever find that whole place in her life where she could smile every day and feel that joy of being blessed with someone who loved her unconditionally.

Before the shower, she hadn't known Tamera well, but now she got a better insight into her. The woman was obviously sentimental, very caring and extremely popular given the number of hugs from guests and lavish gifts from absentees.

One by one the guests trickled out and in the end Kayla, Tamera and Ana were left each holding a glass of champagne. Kayla sat on the floor, her petite legs stretched before her as she leaned against one of the two leather sofas. Tamera sat up on that same sofa with her legs extended across the cushions. Ana lounged across from them with her elbow propped on the arm of the couch, her legs to the side, knees bent.

"If Cole came home now, he'd have a heart attack," Tamera said, twirling her glass and taking in the wreckage of the room.

Ana eyed all the shredded paper, torn ribbons, empty boxes and laughed. "This is like Christmas morning for adults."

"I hope I get a Christmas morning like this." Kayla laughed. "I'm so happy for you two, Tam. My brother is so lucky."

"We're both lucky," Tamera corrected. "I never believed I would find love a second time, let alone with the same man."

Ana had heard bits and pieces of how the two were torn

apart and reunited, but seeing the glow on her face, the sheen in her eyes, really breathed life into the stories.

"Have you ever been in love?" Kayla asked Ana.

"I don't think so." She took a sip of her champagne, not wanting to be the focus of the conversation, especially this one. "I know I've never had feelings like that before."

Both women stared at her. Ana took the silence as her cue to keep going.

"I've had a few relationships, but with my career, it's hard to establish any type of commitment. Besides, I've never found anyone I'd want to have a deeper bond with."

"Until now," Kayla said with her sweet smile.

Ana didn't know how to respond, so Zach's sister's words hung in the air like an unanswered question. Though both women were smiling like they already knew the answer.

Finally Tamera spoke up. "If the man makes you crazy and happy at the same time, if he does unexpected things that are thoughtful and he's expecting nothing in return and he didn't do anything to have to suck up for, then I'd say it's love. Especially if he consumes your thoughts and you instantly feel that flutter of emotions kick in when you hear his voice or see him walking toward you in a crowd."

Ana eased the glass down from her lips and with a shaky hand, sat it on the glass coaster on the low coffee table.

Flutter in the belly. Check.

Thoughtfulness. Check.

Crazy and happy all at once. Check.

Oh, God.

"You don't have to say anything," Tamera said quietly. "And believe me when I tell you we certainly won't tell."

Kayla set down her glass and came to sit next to Ana on the couch. "Oh, honey, don't get upset."

Ana honestly hadn't noticed she was crying until a tear tickled her cheek. "I'm sorry. I honestly just realized it. I mean, I've been wondering if that's what I've been feeling, but hearing you talk about the emotions that come along with love…"

"Zach is a very fortunate man." Tamera smiled. "And I'm sure he feels strongly for you."

Ana shook her head. "No, no. He's made it clear he isn't a relationship kind of guy."

"Maybe not," Kayla agreed, "but I've never seen him go this long without a date or five. He's never let his driver take a woman anywhere that he wasn't there, too, and I can tell you for certain, that he's never, ever looked this happy."

Ana shoved to her feet, pushing through the pile of tissue paper and boxes. "I can't even let myself think like that for a moment. I can't get hurt."

"Love isn't easy." Tamera swung her feet to the floor and sat up. "But it's so worth it in the end. Cole and I went about it the long way. Eleven years later, we're finally getting married. So, if you feel something for Zach, tell him. Don't let time get away. This is your life and you have to take risks now and again to make the most of it."

Just the thought of opening up to Zach made Ana's stomach roll. She had no doubt numerous women had proclaimed their love to him over the years. So what made her so different?

"Don't overanalyze this." Kayla stood, grabbed Ana's hands. "My brother may be known as a ladies' man, but he's got a heart of gold and would never purposely hurt you."

Ana looked Zach's baby sister in the eyes, squeezing her hands. "I know that. It's what he could do without meaning to that scares me."

Fourteen

Zach didn't know what to do about Ana. She was nervous lately. Always talking a mile a minute about nothing in particular.

He hadn't made any more suggestive remarks, hadn't tried to touch her and certainly hadn't allowed himself the luxury of being alone with her.

And it was damn near killing him.

The shower had been a week ago and ever since then, Ana hadn't been herself. He'd asked Kayla and Tamera if something had happened, but they'd both just smiled at him without uttering a word.

Which meant something monumental had occurred and he was more than likely in the center of whatever inside joke these three women were keeping. He shuddered. Nothing was scarier than a woman keeping a secret.

Zach drove his work truck today for the special delivery he had for Miss Anastasia Clark. Sunday was normally his day to relax by his pool, enjoy a beer and think of nothing work-related.

But today he didn't want to relax. Today he wanted to see Ana and to put a genuine smile on her face. He wanted to surprise her, to earn her trust so she would give into this desire that was ready to explode between them.

Zach made a quick stop before he picked up the present for Ana. Once he had all the supplies he needed and the gift sitting next to him in the passenger seat, he headed for her condo.

He couldn't wait to see her face. A part of him was nervous she wouldn't like it or would read too much into the gesture, but he couldn't resist. Ever since she'd opened up about her childhood and her father, he wanted to do something to make her life better.

He hadn't asked, and she hadn't said, if her father had contacted her any more. Zach had already set the plan in motion to take care of Ana's father's debts, with the stipulation that he never contact her or come near her again for any reason. His attorney had drawn up all the necessary legal paperwork, so now he was just waiting until they tracked down the deadbeat to get him to sign.

But he didn't want to bother Ana with that right now. No, today was all about making her smile, seeing her laugh and maybe having her revert to being a child and letting all her worries go for a while.

Zach called Ana's cell when he pulled up to the curb outside her SoBe building.

When she answered, he simply asked, "Busy?"

"No. Why?"

He looked down to the surprise he had waiting for her. "Can you come downstairs? I'm parked right out front."

"Sure," she replied. "Is something wrong?"

"Not at all. But grab your purse or whatever you need because I'm taking you somewhere."

When she paused on the other end, Zach was worried she'd decline. "Um…okay. Give me just a minute."

He disconnected the call, cursing himself for being this anxious over a woman. Since when did he worry about rejection? He'd never been nervous before about presenting a woman with a gift.

Then again, he'd never presented something so personal or hoped to touch any woman's life in such a meaningful way.

Wow. What the hell had happened to him?

Two words. Anastasia Clark.

Within five minutes, the lobby doors whooshed open and Ana stepped through wearing a white tank and cutoff jean shorts with the frayed edges laying against her tanned legs. Her hair was pulled back in a mass of curls.

She looked positively adorable and Zach wanted to gobble her up.

Scooting the surprise over into his lap, he hit the button to unlock the doors.

"You sounded weird on the phone," she said as soon as she opened the passenger door and hopped up into the truck. "You sure nothing's wrong? There wasn't another break-in, was there?"

Without saying a word, he grinned and pulled out the surprise he had hiding between his body and his door.

"Oh, my God!"

"Do you like him?" Zach asked, handing over the furry puppy.

Her entire face softened as she cuddled the black-and-white ball of fuzz to her chest. Lucky dog, he thought.

"Oh, Zach, I love him." She continued to nuzzle her face into the dog's side. "Is he yours? I didn't know you had a puppy."

"I just got him."

Ana smiled. "When I mentioned wanting a dog, you never said you wanted one."

Much as he'd love to sit here and watch her elation, he pulled the truck back out onto the road and headed for home. A place he'd never taken a woman.

"I didn't want a dog," he corrected. "You did. You've mentioned it twice before."

She sat up straighter, turning toward him. "Zach, you can't get a dog because I want one. I can't keep him in the condo. I'm sure they have a policy and I'm not staying forever."

He didn't know why those words bothered him so much.

"He'll stay at my house, but for the duration of this project, he's yours."

Glancing from the road for just a second, he saw Ana biting her bottom lip, tears pooling in her eyes. His grip tightened on the wheel as silence settled in the cab. He didn't want to see gratitude in her eyes, didn't want her to look at him as some type of hero.

"It's no big deal," he told her. "I saw him at the shelter and knew he needed a good home."

"You went to the shelter?"

Zach shrugged. "Yeah, why?"

"I would've taken you for a purebred type."

"Just because I have money doesn't mean I don't remember where I came from." He turned off the freeway. "We were not well-off growing up, Ana. My parents died when we were all barely in high school and we had to work even harder for everything we had when we went to live with my elderly grandmother. There's no reason to give away good money when there are dogs out there who need good homes and someone to love them."

Dear Lord, he thought. All she did was ask about the dog and he turned into a Humane Society infomercial. Why he felt the need to ramble was lost on him. He needed to keep his mouth shut about his personal life and just concentrate on Ana and the fact that she had him all torn up.

While the resort was being erected and moving along swift
nd smooth, his progress with Ana was anything but.

"I don't know what to say," she said, her voice thick
with tears. "I've never had anyone do something so…
houghtful."

Uncomfortable with her emotions, Zach grinned. "How
bout we give him a name?"

"What do you want to name him?" she asked.

"You tell me," he countered. "What would you call him if
e was yours?"

Ana held the little bundle out from her and seemed to study
im. "When I was little I always wanted a big dog and I was
oing to name him Jake."

Zach laughed. "Well, the man at the shelter told me this
og was some sort of a Saint Bernard mix, so he'll get plenty
ig. And Jake sounds like a fine name."

"What do you think?" she asked the dog, once again nuz-
ling her face against his. "Do you like your new name?"

Little squeaky whimpers came from the miniature
uppy.

"I think that's a yes," Zach told her. "I figured we could
o to my house and get him used to his new surroundings."

"What will you do with him when I leave?" Ana asked.

"Keep him, of course. But, for now, consider him yours."

Within minutes he was pulling up his long, palm-lined
Coral Gables driveway. He had to admit, just to himself, that
e wasn't ready to think about Ana leaving. Probably because
e'd always been the one to walk away and he'd never seen the
etreating back of a woman with whom he'd been intimate.

That had to be the reason a lump was forming in his
hroat over this woman and a puppy. Since when did he get
ll emotional?

"Your house is beautiful," Ana said as he pulled in front
f the four-car garage.

He killed the engine and opened his door to get the bags of

supplies from behind his seat. "Thanks. I'm looking for the perfect property to build a place, but I haven't found it yet. I'd like to stay in Miami."

Ana got out with Jake in hand and let him down to sniff his new surroundings. "Why do you want to build something else? This is gorgeous."

Zach glanced at the beige stucco, three-story home with large white columns extending to the second floor where it was topped with a third-floor porch. Yeah, it was nice, but he was ready to move on. Always restless, always ready to find something better. He was done here.

"Want to buy it?" he asked, half joking.

Ana shoved her hands in the pockets of her denim shorts. "I don't need the place I have now, let alone two homes."

Curious, he studied her as she watched the dog follow his nose toward the manicured lawn. "Where do you call home?"

"Well, let's put it this way. I get my mail in a suburb of Chicago. A small cottage that my grandfather willed to me. But I'm rarely there. I use it mostly as my office. I have a secretary who comes in during the day to take calls, make appointments and such, then passes everything along to me."

They followed the dog as he moved around to the side of the house. "Your grandfather built amazing homes and businesses and he still lived in a small cottage?"

Ana smiled up at him. "He was happy and said that's where he'd fallen in love with my grandmother and they had a history there, so he never looked elsewhere. That was just home. I guess that's why I can't bear to sell it."

Zach sighed. Ana was definitely a nostalgic family girl. He certainly appreciated his brother and sister more than anything, but no material thing was that important to him that he wouldn't sell it to obtain something bigger and better.

As they walked around the house, silence settled between

1em and Zach wondered what she was thinking, what she was
:eeling. Did she remember that he'd put the ball in her court
s to whether or not they moved forward in their personal
elationship? The wait was ripping him apart, but he knew
Ana would be worth it. She was special and she was his. For
ow. And even that small epiphany scared the hell out of him.
He'd never been so territorial before.

"You're going to Cole's wedding, right?" he asked.

She looked up at him and shielded her eyes from the sun.
"I hadn't thought about it. Why?"

"It's next weekend." Suddenly Zach wasn't so confident.
Vhy did this woman have that ability to sap his courage?
And why was he holding his breath over his next question?
Would you like to be my date?"

Ana took a step back. "That's not a good idea."

"It's a great idea," he told her, taking a step toward her.
We're working together, spending off-hours together. You've
lready made a great impression on Tamera and Kayla. Why
houldn't you go?"

"The shower was one thing, but a wedding is a personal,
amily-or-close-friend occasion."

Before she could retreat any farther, Zach placed his hands
n her shoulders to stop her. "You are a friend, Ana, and I
vant to get very personal with you."

Yes, he may have thrown down the gauntlet for her weeks
go, but damn if he didn't pick it back up the second his lips
ame down on hers.

He moved his body into hers, wrapping his arms around
er waist and drawing her flush against him. She felt so
erfect, so right. Her arms slid around his neck as he took
dvantage of her mouth by easing her lips apart.

"God, Ana, I want you," he murmured against her
nouth.

She took his face in her hands and stared back at him.

"I know I'm driving you crazy. I'm doing the same thing to myself, but I have to be sure. Can you understand that?"

Having been a risk taker his entire life, no, he didn't understand, but he was willing to try. For her. He could see the desire in her eyes and knew that he could have her now if he pressed enough. But what would that get him? An evening of hot, sweaty sex? No, when he finally got Ana, he wanted more than one night to explore, to teach, to worship.

And he didn't want her to second-guess herself the entire time. He wanted her to come to him with total abandonment.

"Come to the wedding with me."

She kissed him, softly, tenderly. "Okay." Then she eased back. "Now what do you say we take Jake inside and get him fed?"

Zach smiled. He'd never had to plead for a date before, but he'd also never felt this good about one.

Ana was seriously the equivalent of every business deal he'd ever had. The ones he truly appreciated were the ones he worked hardest to get.

Cole's wedding couldn't get here soon enough. Once the wedding was over, the reception finished, Zach knew Ana wouldn't deny him. Not with an ambiance of love surrounding them and the fact that family and a select few of their friends were invited to stay at the Star Island home afterward.

Less than a week and Zach was sure Ana would take what he'd been offering.

Zach couldn't push his Harley fast enough. Finally an arrest had been made in the breaking and entering at the construction site over a month ago and seeing as how he hadn't been by yet to check on progress today, he decided to tell Ana in person.

He always got excited when he pulled onto the private property that led to the resort. The skeletal frame had been done, but in Zach's eye, he could already see the completed masterpiece.

Of course, he also got a little thrill when he pulled onto the site because of a certain sexy, albeit frustrating forewoman who always looked amazing in her little tanks and hard hat.

He was surprised to not find her out with the crew, so he made his way into her office. Empty. Zach went back out and was approached by a member of Ana's crew.

"She's not here, Mr. Marcum," the sweat-covered man said. "We had to call the ambulance—"

"Ambulance?" Panic flooded through every single part of his body. "Is she hurt? Did she fall?"

"Dehydrated," the man said. "The squad just left with her about ten minutes ago. Damn hot out here and she's always too busy making sure we all have enough water, I suppose she forgot to get some herself."

"If you need anything, call my cell," Zach said, running back to his bike. "I'm going to the E.R. now."

Not waiting around for another moment to pass him by, Zach brought the engine to life and made record time in reaching the hospital. Damn fool woman. How many times had he told her the Miami heat was nothing like what she was used to?

Anger, worry, fear, they all accompanied him to the doors of the E.R. And even though Zach knew her condition wasn't life threatening, he still couldn't get to her fast enough.

Once he told a little lie that he was family, the nurse let him into the room.

Ana, still in her white tank, cutoff denim shorts and dusty boots, was hooked up to an IV. She looked up from where a nurse drew her blood and rolled her eyes.

"Seriously? They called you to come down here?"

Zach stepped farther into the room and pulled the curtain behind him. "No, I was on my way to talk to you and one of the crew members told me what happened."

"I don't want to hear it," she told him, then hissed as the nurse pricked her delicate arm with a needle to draw blood. "I know to drink and stay hydrated, but I'm a little too tired right now to argue. Can we just say you were right and move on?"

Zach laughed and moved to the other side of her bed. "You must be tired if you can't argue with me."

"Okay, Miss Clark." The nurse tossed the trash and gathered her things. "The doctor will be in shortly."

"Wonderful." Ana sighed and settled into the bed. "What did you need to tell me?" she asked him.

"What? Oh, nothing that can't wait." He just wanted to look at her. Wanted to make sure she was really okay because when that initial shock of her being taken away by an ambulance had hit him, he'd imagined the worst.

Ana closed her eyes, clasped her hands over her flat stomach. Zach hated to see the IV sticking from her delicate wrist.

"I'm not going anywhere," she told him. "You might as well tell me what you needed to say then you can go."

He took one of her hands and nestled it between his. "I'm not going anywhere."

Opening her eyes, she turned her head and smiled. "I'm fine, Zach. I'm just going to lie here, get some more fluids and I'll be good as new in a couple of hours."

He returned her gaze, leaving no room for argument. "I'm staying."

"Then tell me what you wanted to say."

"An arrest was made in the break-in."

She sat up, her eyes wide now. "Who did they arrest?"

"Nate. Claims he was mad and wanted to teach you a lesson."

"Arrogant jerk. What took the cops so long to arrest him?"

"He'd fled the state. Victor and I had an investigator hunt him down. Nate was picked up in Michigan."

Ana gritted her teeth. "Too bad the investigator couldn't accidentally have shot him. Then we wouldn't have to worry about pressing charges."

Zach laughed, brought her tiny hand up to his lips. "Bloodthirsty, aren't you? He's going to go before a jury and pay for his crime."

"Probably with a slap on the wrist."

Feeling more confident, Zach eased down on the edge of the narrow bed. "Seriously, stop worrying about it. Don't worry about anything. Not the break-in, not your father or the divorce, and not even the resort. I can't believe I just said that."

Ana laughed. Just the response he was looking for. "Okay, Dr. Marcum. I am tired. I'm just going to close my eyes for a second. Okay?"

He nodded and continued to stare long after her breathing slowed. When the nurse came in to change the bag of fluids, Zach still remained on the edge of the bed clutching her hand. When the doctor came in to order more blood work to make sure her levels were back up, Zach thanked him.

Funny. He couldn't recall any woman in his past, other than his sister, with whom he would've sat for hours in an E.R. over something this minor.

Come to think of it, there were a lot of things he'd do for Ana that he wouldn't have done for past lovers. And that was the funniest part of all. Anastasia Clark wasn't even his lover.

Fifteen

Tonight was the night.

It was all Ana could think of as she stepped into the lobby to wait for Zach to pick her up. She took a deep, calming breath but her heart still fluttered.

She'd known from the moment she'd told him that she would be his date for his brother's wedding that she would give herself to Zach tonight. There was no denying him, or herself, anymore.

The jumble of flurries in her belly stemmed from pure excitement from the promises the evening held. She had no expectations, no thoughts as to what she wanted to get out of a night with Zach. At such a monumental moment in her life, she knew she had to take each step at a time and follow her heart.

Ana clutched her gold handbag and stared at her reflection in the lobby doors. She was so glad she'd let Kayla take her shopping for a dress to wear to the wedding. The shimmering emerald strapless matched her eyes, and Kayla had assured Ana that Zach would not be able to take his eyes off her.

Ana had even gone to great lengths to tame her mass of curls by going to the salon several hours ago. Now her hair was smoothed to a shine and tumbled down her back in soft waves. She'd never have been able to achieve this look on her own, so she'd tipped the stylist very well.

But as Ana continued to study her reflection, she wondered if maybe she should've chosen the short, gold dress with straps instead of this floor-length strapless.

A limo pulled up and Ana quit fussing with her dress and hair. Even though she was anxious, she needed to stay calm and just enjoy what life was so graciously offering.

She just hoped Zach still wanted her once he saw her. She did look different, and not just the hair. Her makeup was heavier than she normally wore, as well. Would he like the bronzed shimmer that she'd used to highlight her shoulders? Would he appreciate the brand-new lingerie she'd purchased just that morning with him in mind?

The limo driver opened the rear door and Zach emerged looking sexy, sinful and perfect in an all-black suit. The best man would look even more dashing than the groom. Of course, that was her own opinion.

She knew when he spotted her. Zach froze. With nothing between them but the glass doors, Ana could only stare in return. She didn't think having a conversation with only your eyes was possible, but she'd been wrong before.

Zach's traveling gaze over her body may as well have been his big, strong hands. Ana tilted her head, smiled and spun in a slow circle with her arms out, sending him a subtle signal that this was all his for the taking. Later. Another shiver of delight speared through her. She only hoped her newfound bravery held up through the night.

Ana walked through the sliding doors. "I'm glad you didn't bring one of the bikes."

"I'm glad you decided to go with me." He ran a fingertip across her bare collarbone. "Damn, you're sexy. Every man there will want you."

"But I'm yours."

His hand froze on her heated skin. "Ana…"

She stepped closer, leaning in to his ear so the driver and valets couldn't hear. "For tonight, I'm yours. I don't want to think about how different we are, or that in a few months we'll part ways. Tonight, Zach, take what you want."

As she eased back, she saw Zach swallow. And for once, since she'd known him, he was speechless.

Zach turned toward the open door to the car and assisted her, following her in before the driver closed the door.

"I always thought you were beautiful," he whispered, taking her hand in his. "But I had no idea you could be so stunning that my mind could actually go blank."

"Kayla helped me," Ana confessed. "She took me shopping for the dress and I went to the salon for my hair."

His eyes settled on her shadowed cleavage. "Remind me to get Kayla a very nice birthday present next month."

Ana laughed. "If you don't stop, we won't be able to get out of the car at the wedding."

He lifted a brow. "Is that a bad thing?"

"It wouldn't look good if the best man didn't show." She laughed. "Try to control yourself."

"You're kidding, right?"

Ana shrugged. "Just think about what good behavior will get you. Oh, and try to picture what I'm wearing under this."

Zach groaned and squeezed her hand. "You sure you've never done this before? You're too good at torture."

Nerves swirled around Ana's belly. "I promise. I've been waiting on the right person. Are you sure you want to be with someone who may do everything wrong?"

Zach shifted in the seat, took her other hand in his as

well. "You will do nothing wrong. We'll do this together and nothing could be more perfect. Relax."

Relax? Sure. No problem. She only had several hours to go knowing that this man was going to bring out a new side of herself tonight and they would explore that side together.

Relaxing should be no problem. Right?

Standing up as best man was pure agony seeing as how he kept looking into the crowd to make eye contact with Ana.

He wanted to be alone. With her. Now.

But as his twin and Tamera said their vows, he had to look away from Ana. She was tearing up and smiling like women do at weddings. She was no doubt wondering what her own wedding would be like someday.

And Zach instantly loathed the faceless man who would take Ana and make her his for life.

If Zach were looking to settle down—the thought was laughable—he would certainly explore where this desire with Ana would go. But he wasn't, so he would take what she offered tonight and not worry about anything else.

"You may kiss the bride," the minister said.

Finally. Zach clapped along with the other one hundred fifty guests as Cole and Tamera kissed and turned to be introduced as Mr. and Mrs. Cole Marcum.

As the sun set in the background and flocks of doves were released to fly overhead, Zach smiled. This sort of fanfare wasn't for him. But he was so happy for his brother and new sister-in-law. Happy they'd found each other and wanted to share their love with so many people.

After the receiving line was finished, Zach went in search of Ana to make sure she was okay and not feeling lonely since he had duties to see to as the best man. But once that toast was over, he was skipping out of this shindig early and taking Ana upstairs to one of the numerous guest rooms to make love to her all night.

Make love? Whoa. Where the hell did that come from? He'd never thought of sex as making love.

Must be all the holy matrimony getting to his head.

"You next?"

Zach spun around to see Victor Lawson smiling, a glass of champagne in hand.

"Hardly," Zach replied. "What about you?"

"Married? No, thanks. Too busy enjoying life." He motioned with his drink toward Tamera and Cole. "But love looks good on them."

"Yes, it does."

Zach glanced at the happy couple, then allowed his eyes to wander until he spotted Ana. All the breath left his lungs. Those mesmerizing deep green eyes were on him, half shielded by heavy lids.

And she had the same look in her eye as she looked at him that Tamera had when Cole had said his vows.

No, no, no. She couldn't be in love. Could she?

And why, when Victor mentioned love and marriage, did he automatically seek Ana?

All this wedded bliss was wreaking havoc on his mind, making him weak and vulnerable. Time to make a quick exit.

"If you'll excuse me," Zach said, nodding to Victor.

A wide grin spread across the billionaire's face. "I don't blame you for the interest in Miss Clark. She's got that quiet, reserved beauty, but knows how to make a statement when it counts. Makes a man want to take notice."

Zach didn't return the smile. "So long as *you* don't take notice, we'll get along just fine."

Victor's chuckle followed and mocked Zach across the courtyard. He didn't care. All that concerned him was Ana and the fact that she was ready to give him the greatest gift he'd ever received.

Cole may be the one to have gotten married, but Zach considered himself the luckiest man here tonight.

When he reached her side, she was chatting with some guests. He softly took her elbow and whispered in her ear, "Let's go."

The tremor that shook her also vibrated through him. Ana graciously said her farewells and allowed him to lead her back into the house.

"Did you at least tell Cole and Tamera goodbye?" she asked as they passed the marble entryway and headed toward the wide, curved staircase.

"They left an hour ago," he told her. "They were eager to be alone, too."

Instead of going up the stairs as he'd originally planned, Zach led her out the front door.

"Where are we going?" she asked. "I thought we were staying here tonight. Isn't that what Cole had planned for the family and close friends?"

He led her to his Camaro, which he'd had Cole's driver bring over, and opened the passenger door, but before she could settle into the seat, he turned her around, pinned her against the car and kissed her. Gentleness had no place here, not right now when he was ready to explode. He would be gentle later when she needed it most.

Before he could get carried away right here in the driveway, Zach eased back, but kept his body flush with hers so she would know how affected he was.

"This matters to me," he murmured against her moist lips. "I want you in my bed and I want privacy."

When he stepped back to let her have room to get in the car, she continued to stare. "Are you always this passionate?"

Her honest, whispered question took him by surprise, but he didn't even have to think. "I can honestly say I've never felt this way before."

Ana closed her eyes, sighed. "Don't say things like that to me."

He didn't know what she meant by that or why she looked so torn, so he just gestured for her to get into the car.

Months ago he was so confident, so sure he would have her in his bed. Of course at that time he didn't literally intend to have her at his home, his sanctuary. He'd planned on seducing her aboard his yacht, maybe whisking her off to his cabin in the hills of Tennessee for extra seclusion. Or maybe just a quick evening romp in her on-site office after hours.

Yeah, he'd been cocky and sure of himself. But as he settled in behind the driver's seat, Zach was hit by an attack of nerves like he'd never experienced before.

Ana was innocent and that meant this evening would be a first for him as well.

Surprisingly Ana didn't feel as nervous as she thought she'd be at this moment she'd dreamed of. If anything, she felt a sense of peace, like she was doing something right. As Zach pulled into his four-car garage and killed the engine, silence enveloped them.

Yes, she'd waited a long time to give herself to a man, but she wasn't sorry she was going to give herself to Zach. She loved him, and he cared for her as much as he could. Once upon a time, Ana wouldn't have accepted that. Not that she was settling now, not by any means. She'd never been in love before, but she was now. Was it her fault her heart chose someone who was skittish of love? He had every reason to be considering his ex had skipped out on him in such a swift, coldhearted way.

Ana opened her car door before Zach could. They walked by two of his motorcycles and the Jag and the Bugatti and finally stepped into the house, where he promptly turned off the alarm.

"Where's Jake?" she asked, setting her purse on the island in the kitchen.

"He's in the crate. I'd better let him out to do his business before…"

Ana smiled as Zach trailed off and went into the utility room to let out their dog.

Their dog. No way could Zach deny that he loved her. Oh, he may not be ready to admit it, but deep down he did. Otherwise he never would've gotten her a gift so meaningful. He wouldn't have remembered her even mentioning that in her rambling comments about her family.

Yes, Zach Marcum may be resistant when it came to commitments and relationships, but they hadn't even made love and he hadn't seen another woman in months.

That spoke volumes in ways his words couldn't. And solidified the fact that giving herself to him was not a mistake or something she would regret later. Even if they went their separate ways after the project was finished, Zach would always have a piece of her heart.

"Would you like a drink?"

Ana spun around as Zach reentered the room. "No, thanks. Did you already let Jake out?"

He nodded. "I put him on the enclosed patio. There are puppy pads for him and not much those little sharp teeth can tear up out there. Plus it gives him some room to walk around after being cooped up for several hours."

Ana walked through the kitchen and into the living area where a large flat screen TV was framed to look like a picture between floor-to-ceiling bookshelves.

The stark white walls were tastefully adorned with pictures of various sailboats out on the ocean. He also had a pencil sketch of a sailboat on an easel in the corner. The lone drawing drew her interest.

"You like sailboats?" She glanced over her shoulder to where he remained at the entryway just watching her. "I didn't pay attention to all these the other day when we brought Jake here. Guess I was too busy playing with him."

"Well, that just boosts my ego. You notice them now when I'm dying to strip you out of that dress?"

She turned fully now, more than aware of her heart beating, her palms sweating. Okay, maybe she was more nervous than she thought. "I actually have never been on the water. Too busy working, I guess."

He moved toward her, one slow step at a time, and her heart picked up its pace. Game on. Let the predator come to his prey.

"You sketched this?" she asked, turning back to the drawing before he reached her. "Your talents are endless with design."

His warm breath hit her bare shoulder as his words caressed her skin mere inches from her ear. "Are we really standing here discussing how well I draw? I have many, many more talents, Anastasia, and I want to show them all to you."

She turned, her breasts brushing against his crisp dress shirt. Yes, she wanted this man and it thrilled her beyond description that he wanted her, but she'd be a fool not to go into this with a bit of fear.

"Relax, Zach." She smiled, laying a hand on his chest. "I'm not going anywhere. Even though I'm nervous and scared, I need this to go slow. Can you handle that?"

He rested his hands on her bare shoulders, extending his thumbs down to brush against the tops of her breasts spilling from the dress. "I've watched you move all night in that dress. I've watched other men look at you and each minute that passed was too long for me not to touch you. But I don't want to scare you. I want to show you how perfect this will be. Let me show you, Ana."

Ana didn't protest when his hands slid around to her back and eased the zipper down. Emerald silk swished to the floor in utter silence.

And the look in Zach's eyes was so worth the extra money she'd put toward her new lingerie. How could she make this as good and perfect for Zach as he'd promised it would be for her? She knew nothing about pleasuring a man. But the look in his eyes told her she was about to learn very soon.

Shivers of anticipation swept through her and in their path excitement and love now replaced fear.

Sixteen

More than anything Zach wanted to run his hands all over Ana's slender body, but he knew the moment he touched her smooth skin, this night would progress at a much faster pace than he wanted. And right now, he wanted to savor this moment with his eyes and capture a mental picture of every dip, every curve of her body.

"The dress was stunning," he said, almost not recognizing his own husky voice. "But this is positively breathtaking."

A wide grin spread across her face. "I was hoping you'd like what I chose."

Wrapping a body like Ana's in clothes should be a sin. But wrapping it in a sheer gold thong and bustier was pure heaven.

"I'm glad you like it, Zach, but could you touch me or start taking off some clothes? I feel a little silly being on display."

He jerked his shirt from his pants and unbuttoned it, tossing it over his shoulder, not caring one bit where it landed.

Zach wrapped his arms around her waist, pulling her against his chest. They matched perfectly. Chest to chest, stomach to stomach, thighs to thighs.

"I don't get to give you the microscopic overview?" she asked, teasing.

"Later."

He bent down, scooped her up and made his way out of the living room, through the wide, long hallway and toward the front of the house where his master suite was located. The whole east side of his home was his bedroom, his domain, and he wanted to spend the next two days closed in with nothing and no one but Ana and her innocence.

He eased her down to her stiletto-covered feet. "Be sure, Anastasia."

She ran the palm of her hands over his bare chest, never taking her eyes off his. Slowly she eased her body closer, until her lips were a breath from his, and smiled. When her arms looped around his neck, she gave him a gentle tug until he was walking her backward toward the high four-poster bed dominating the center of the massive room.

She sank down on the edge as he towered over her. Pure, raw heat shimmered in her green eyes. The mass of red hair, usually curly and wild, was now tamed and tumbling down her back. He couldn't wait to see it spread across his sheets.

Ana licked her lips, but not in the suggestive way most women did. Her eyes darted to the ground, then back up.

That she was getting nervous humbled him. A surreal feeling, but one he was learning to live with considering Ana had become a part of his life he hadn't expected.

More than anything, he wanted to make this night, this moment perfect for her. He wanted to ruin her for any other man.

No. Those thoughts had to leave. There was only room in this bed for two. And he refused to already give her up to someone else, even if only in his mind.

Zach placed a hand on either side of her hips on the bed and leaned down to capture her mouth. Tipping her face up, she rose to meet him. She sighed deeply as she opened her mouth, giving him access. Her back arched, the satiny material over her breasts brushing against his bare chest.

Taking her shoulders, he eased her down and placed a knee on the bed. As much as he wanted to continue kissing her, he wanted to see her completely free of all clothing first. He knew he needed to take his time, something he'd never had to consider before, but he didn't know how agonizing it would be. He wanted to draw this moment out for both of them.

With one knee on the bed, one foot on the floor, Zach eased back and began unfastening the little hook and eye closures on her bustier. One by one they popped open, exposing creamy, pale skin beneath.

"You make me feel beautiful," she whispered.

Zach's eyes roamed up to Ana's. "You should never feel any other way."

He parted the shiny material, laying it open on either side of her torso. Then he hooked his thumbs in the side strings of her panties and slid them down her slender legs, over the heels and flung them off.

Laid bare before him, in his own bed, Ana looked like sin personified. Those mesmerizing eyes sparkled, her chest heaved with every breath she took. Her moist lips were parted, begging him to take more.

To know he was looking at a body that had never been touched, never been admired nearly brought him to his knees.

"I've always taken this for granted," he told her as he ran his hands up her legs, over her pelvic bone and up to her breasts. "You have no idea what you do to me, Ana."

She sat up, reached for his belt and unfastened it along with the button and zipper of his pants. "I know, Zach. I know because you do the same to me."

Once his pants were off, along with his socks and shoes, he bent to take off her killer heels. Now that she was fully naked, he kissed his way from her feet to her breasts, bypassing her most sacred part.

She wiggled and moaned beneath his touch. Zach wanted nothing more than to bury himself in her and assuage this ache he had, but he was realistic. He knew that with Ana once would never be enough. No, once she got into his system, he had a feeling it would be hard to ever get over her.

Concentrating on the here and now, he took one nipple into his mouth. When her back arched off the bed, he wrapped both arms around her waist to hold her closer. And that was another first for him. He couldn't get close enough or touch her enough. He literally couldn't wait to become one with her.

Zach turned his attention to the other nipple, then traveled up her neck and finally reclaimed her mouth. Ana grabbed his shoulders, her short nails biting into his skin as she lifted her knees around him.

He trailed one hand down her body, found the spot between her legs and stroked. He needed to make sure she was ready, and not just emotionally.

Ana's mouth tore from his as she cried out at his touch. He couldn't wait another minute. He grabbed his pants off the floor and pulled a condom from his wallet.

"Look at me," he told her as he positioned himself between her legs. "Don't ever forget this moment."

Don't forget me, he silently added.

Inch by agonizing inch, he entered her. Their eyes stayed locked as Zach allowed her body to adjust.

Ana brought her hands up to his cheeks, framing his face in between her fingers. "Please, Zach. Don't hold back."

He didn't. "Wrap your legs around my waist."

When she did, he sheathed himself in her even deeper. Her

hips tilted with each thrust and Zach had to grit his teeth to remain in control.

"I'm so glad it's you," she murmured right before she gripped the duvet in each of her fists, threw her head back and came beneath him. That's all it took for Zach to let go.

And as much as he wanted her to remember this moment, he wanted to keep it embedded in his own head forever, so he leaned down and kissed her as his body trembled and even when the tremors ceased.

Sated, Ana kept her eyes closed. She was afraid if she opened them she'd see this was a dream. Or worse, Zach was disappointed.

He shifted his body over and she instantly felt the loss of his presence, but in an instant he was lying at her side again, trailing his fingertips over her heated body.

"Are you okay?" he asked.

Ana smiled, opened her eyes and turned her head toward him. "I can't believe I'm in your bed. I never thought this would make me feel so...alive."

The look on his face was sexy, yet at the same time vulnerable. The words I love you settled on the tip of her tongue. She wanted to tell him how she felt, but she didn't want this moment to turn into guilt on his part. He wouldn't be able to say the words in return and he would probably think she was just saying it because of what had just happened.

So she kept the secret for another time. But she would tell him. Soon. He deserved to know how he'd touched her life, how he would always be a part of her even if they weren't together.

He broke the silence. "I have to say, these last few hours of you in that dress really tested a man's willpower."

She laughed, rolling to her side and mimicking his pose. With her elbow bent and her head resting in her hand, she looked at him. "It was just a dress, Zach. I'm the same person in my dusty boots and holey jeans as I was in that dress."

His brows drew together. "That's what I'm trying to figure out. How can someone look so totally different, yet amazingly sexy both ways?"

"I don't know. Why don't you tell me? You go from a CEO to a construction worker to a motorcycle rider in a flash."

His wide grin split across his face, making that stubbled jawline all the more appealing. "Are you saying we're not that different? I'm positive I wouldn't have looked that good in the dress."

Ana laughed and shoved him in his chest until he fell to his back. She came up on her knees, still laughing, took a pillow and smacked him. "Now you're making fun."

"Maybe just a little."

Zach clasped his hands behind his head, instinctively flexing those hard muscles in his arms, accentuating his tribal-looking tattoo that wrapped around one hefty bicep.

How could she not have fallen hard for this man? All that sex appeal wrapped around the heart of a true gentleman. He could have anyone, yet he'd taken time to earn her trust, show her what passion and, yes, love was. All the afterglow, all the tingling feelings swirling around inside her, and all of the confidence she had in herself were all due to Zach.

How in the world had she ever thought this caring, giving man was anything like her selfish, womanizing father?

"What are you thinking?" he asked, gazing up at her.

She shrugged, came to sit on her knees, surprising herself at just how comfortable she was naked in his bed. "Everything. Nothing."

"You were smiling, but you had a different look in your eye for a second." He rested a big, tanned hand against her pale thigh. "What was it?"

"I love you."

Silence settled so deep into the room, Ana wanted to be buried in it. "Oh, God. I told myself I wouldn't tell you."

She covered her face with her hands, praying the last ten seconds of her life would be erased from Zach's memory.

"Ana." The bed shifted as Zach sat up and took her hands in his. "Look at me."

Slowly moving her hands, she looked him in the eye. But he wasn't horrified. At least he didn't appear to be.

"I'm sure you hear that all the time," she began, suddenly trying to backpedal in a current too forceful for her to fight. "And I'm not just saying it because we made love. I told myself not to say anything, to just let this moment be and not bring my personal emotions into it. But, much as I want to, I can't take the words back. I know you don't feel the same, and I'm fine with that. I knew going in that you wouldn't love me."

He remained motionless as she rambled, except for the one corner of his sexy mouth that turned up into a smile. "Are you finished?"

Ana shook her head. "I tried not to fall for you. I really did, Zach. But do you know how much you've done for me?"

"Excuse me?" His brows drew together. "I didn't do anything."

"You gave my company this amazing job." She began ticking the list off on her fingers. "You were there for me when my office was broken into. When my father showed up, you stood by my side. You've been so patient with me even though I know that goes against everything you've probably ever done where a woman was concerned. And Jake. You gave me a dog, Zach. Something I wanted when I was a little girl and you just delivered it to me."

"Let me get this straight," he said, still holding on to her hands. "You love me because I was in the right place for the break-in and your father's visit and because I got a dog?"

Ana closed her eyes. "That is all on the surface," she whispered, knowing tears weren't far. She opened her eyes anyway, not caring she was baring all the emotion there. "You gave me a sense of hope that not all men are jerks. That not all men who can literally have it all are uncaring and selfish. You put me first, in everything. I don't think you know what that means to me."

"Ana." Zach sighed. "I don't know what to say. I do care about you. I can't even try to deny that. But…"

She'd be lying if she said a piece of her heart hadn't just chipped away. There was never any question that he wouldn't fall in love with her, but she was hoping for just a sliver of his love.

"I don't expect you to say anything," she told him. "But I can't lie to you, Zach. I'm not sorry you know how I feel. So, now that I've embarrassed myself, can we enjoy the rest of the evening or did I ruin it?"

He leaned in, touched his lips lightly to hers. "Never."

Thankful he wasn't terrified of her now, Ana smiled. "I bet you'll never ask me again what I'm thinking."

Zach slid off the bed and scooped her up into a fireman's carry. "Not for a while, I won't."

As he carried her into the glass-tiled bathroom, Ana couldn't help but smile. The words of affection were out now and she felt relieved. Scared, but relieved.

And now that the truth was out in the open, would he, could he consider something more with Ana than a fling? God, how she hoped so. She wanted desperately to see where this love could go. If only Zach would open his eyes, and his heart.

Seventeen

Zach had just finished sliding the pancakes onto a large platter when his cell rang. He grabbed it from the kitchen island praying it wasn't Melanie again. She'd left him three texts during the night, all of which he'd ignored and deleted.

Thankfully it wasn't her. It was his attorney.

"Zach, we've found Miss Clark's father."

He glanced toward the arched doorway to make sure Ana hadn't wandered in from the bedroom. He'd left her sleeping and decided to make her a surprise breakfast in bed.

"He agreed to sign the contract?" Zach asked. "That was too easy."

"Well, an IRS threat really scares people into doing what you'd like," his lawyer agreed. "All debts, legal and otherwise, are clear. Everything is taken care of."

Zach could feel the relief lifting off his shoulders. Now when he and Ana parted, he would know she could move on without that extra baggage and could live without fear. But he would have to keep his investigator on this for a while, just to make sure Ana's father held up his end of the bargain. Zach had a feeling the man would, simply because people like that were too afraid of people with power. He would slink into someone else's life and start anew with some other innocent.

"Thanks," Zach said. "Make sure you let the P.I. know how much he is appreciated and that a hefty bonus will be added to his fees for his swift, efficient work. And make sure he knows to keep an eye on Miss Clark once this project is complete. I don't want her or her mother bothered with this bastard anymore."

He disconnected the call and pulled the syrup from the cabinet. Now he could greet Ana with a simple breakfast of pancakes and juice, a morning-after kiss and the good news about her father who would no longer be a problem in her life.

Zach loaded up the tray and headed back to the bedroom. Ana was just rustling beneath the covers.

"Morning." He smiled and moved toward her with the tray. "I hope you like pancakes."

She stretched, arms high above her head, and pulled the covers back up and tucked them beneath her arms. "You know I love food, so anything is fine."

He settled the tray over her lap and leaned down to kiss her. "I like to see a woman who's not afraid to eat."

Ana's wide grin spread across her face. "I've told you, you date the wrong women."

Something settled deep in Zach's chest at her subtle joke. "I'm beginning to see that," he mumbled against her mouth before capturing it again.

He couldn't explore his emotions, not now. Maybe never. This uncomfortable state that had been plaguing him for days, weeks, was confusing him, making him lose track of what was right before him.

Zach took the kiss deeper, and Ana cupped his face and parted her lips. How could he ever let this woman out of his bed? Out of his life? Was he seriously contemplating something long-term?

Zach pulled back, more than a little shaken at the smack to the heart from the sudden epiphany. "Eat before they get cold," he told her.

"Aren't you eating?"

He shook his head. "I had some juice and fruit while your pancakes were cooking."

Placing the napkin in her lap, Ana picked up the syrup and drizzled it over her plate. "You seem off. Is everything okay?"

"Fine." Zach eased down on the edge of the bed. "Just conducted some business this morning. I wasn't expecting to wrap it up this fast."

"You're all work, Zach." She cut into the pancake and lifted a forkful to her mouth. "I thought you were only working on the Lawson project right now."

"This was something that couldn't wait." Zach scooted farther back on the bed and turned to face her more. "I'm glad it's done and came through quicker than I'd expected."

"So you can spend more time on…more important things."

Zach smiled and leaned closer. "Absolutely," he said, moving over the tray to capture her mouth.

He wanted her to know how much she meant to him, but at the same time he couldn't tell her because she would read too much into it.

Zach eased back. "Finish eating. We can take Jake out to play later and let him run some energy off."

"Can I grab a quick shower first?"

"Absolutely. You don't have to ask to use anything here."

Zach left Ana to go into his office on the other side of the house. He wanted to read the contract that his attorney had faxed to make sure there were no loopholes Ana's father could jump through in the future.

Everything had to be in order down to the final period if he expected to move on. And he would move on. He had to. As soon as Ana was one-hundred-percent safe.

By the time he read over the document, he was more than satisfied that his lawyer hadn't missed a thing. Of course, he had expected no less, but he wasn't going to take even the slightest chance when it came to Ana's future.

Zach filed the contract in his cabinet and strode back to his bedroom. He heard the shower shut off just as he grabbed the tray. He took the empty dishes back to the kitchen and left them on the counter. His housekeeper would be in later.

When he went back to his bedroom, Ana still hadn't emerged from the bathroom. He'd just raised a hand to knock when the door whipped open.

Ana's face was tear streaked and she'd donned his black silk robe that hung on the back of the door. Instincts took control as he stepped forward and grasped her shoulders.

"What's wrong?"

She shook her head and brushed by him. "Absolutely nothing. Everything is perfect. That's the problem."

Zach turned, watching Ana pace back and forth across his white carpet. "You've lost me. You found a problem in my bathroom?"

She stopped, hands on her hips, a mass of wet, red hair settling around her shoulders. "No. I'm just so happy and I started feeling guilty while I was enjoying your party-size shower. I don't think my mother experienced an ounce of the happiness I've had in the past few weeks. And that makes me sad."

Treading into unfamiliar territory, Zach took a hesitant step forward. This was a shaky part where every word he said could give her false hope for a future. "Ana, don't feel guilty. I can't imagine your mother would want you to. I'm sure she'd want you to be happy."

Ana's shoulders relaxed, her hands fell to her sides and her head drooped. "I know she would. Which is what makes her so great. She always puts others first. I wish my father would've appreciated what he had and what he's thrown away. He used his power to get anything and everything and where's it gotten him?"

"I won't lie and say money doesn't talk, but people with power can't let the power overtake their lives." Feeling a bit more in control of this shaky situation, Zach closed the gap between them and placed his hands on her silk-covered shoulders. "Money and power have ruined many lives. You have to think more of yourself and be stronger than the power…if that makes sense."

Ana looked at him as one tear trickled down each cheek. "If I didn't love you before, I love you now."

"Ana, I can't…"

Her smile broke his heart. "I know," she whispered, slipping her thumbs inside his boxers and sliding them down his legs. "Let me show you."

The loose knot she'd tied at her waist came free with just one slight tug. She dropped her arms to her sides as he brushed the robe from her shoulders.

She moved into him, wrapping her arms around his neck and kissing his stubbled jawline. He circled his hands around her waist and groaned at the slow pace she was dead set on keeping.

"Don't ever doubt my feelings for you," she whispered in his ear. "And don't lie to yourself."

The little minx knew exactly what she was doing because just as he was about to ask what she was talking about, she covered his mouth with hers and ran her hands down his sides and around to his back where she massaged him from bottom to top.

"Enough," he rasped.

Zach wrapped his arms around her waist, picked her up and walked over to the chaise in front of his French doors which he'd opened at sunrise. The ocean breeze slipped through, kissing their bare bodies.

Once he had Ana laid out, ready for him, Zach made quick work of protection and came back to stand between her legs. With no words, no kissing, he entered her. A moment later he stopped.

"Don't stop," she told him. "Don't doubt."

He clenched his teeth. "I can't control myself around you, Anastasia. I can't give you slow."

"Then don't."

When she smiled, looking up at him with desire in her heavy-lidded eyes, he was a goner. He leaned over, bracing himself with one hand on the arm of the chaise, one hand at Ana's side, and moved with her.

Desire overtook him and just as he was about to close his eyes, he saw hers. Nothing but love looked up at him and Zach knew if he could love anyone, it would be Ana. He wanted nothing more than to make her happy but he was broken and not willing to take the risk again.

So he closed his eyes and took them both over the edge.

When Ana came back to reality and Zach dropped her off at her condo, she discovered four messages on her cell from her mother.

She'd been so busy enjoying herself between the amazing wedding, the reception, but mostly the hours after. Had she really only spent less than twenty-four hours with Zach? So much had happened since she'd last been in her bedroom.

Her whole life had changed—not to mention her outlook on life.

She'd told herself, once she decided to sleep with Zach, that he wouldn't expect anything in return…. And she wouldn't have if he hadn't looked at her the same way she'd seen Cole look at Tamera.

A burst of giddiness swept through her at the fact that Zach may actually love her. She'd wondered before, but now she had a bit more hope. When they'd been one and he'd looked into her eyes, she'd seen the emotion as clearly as if he'd said the words. She seriously didn't think she was imagining things just because her own feelings were out there.

As Ana listened to her mother's messages, her excitement increased. Her mother wanted to come for a visit and to see how the new project was coming along.

Nearly six months had passed since Ana had seen her mother. She couldn't wait to show her how the site was progressing. Maybe she could stay until the end of the project since she was technically single and had no job to be home for.

Oh, who was Ana kidding? She was more excited about Zach and her mother meeting. Of course, that was a giant step into relationship territory and she didn't want to stress Zach or make him feel trapped, but she did want him to see another side of her. And she wanted her mother to meet the one man who'd touched Ana so deeply, he'd be embedded into her heart forever.

Ana called her mother and made arrangements for her to fly in on Friday. That would give her time to get Zach used to the idea of her mother's arrival.

And even though the proverbial "meeting of the parents" was a giant step in a relationship, Ana couldn't let this opportunity pass her by.

She sank down on her bed and stared out the wide window toward the harbor. Taking on this project had changed her life in so many unpredictable ways. How would she cope with leaving Miami? Would Zach want her to stay? They still had many months to go before she could pack up and go. Surely in that time he would be honest with himself.

Ana knew, at this point, the best thing she could do was just be herself. After all, she hadn't done anything to get Zach to have feelings for her, so she certainly wasn't pressing her luck by making him open up about something he feared.

No, this was a monumental decision and one Zach needed to come to on his own. And if he didn't, well, when she left and said goodbye for the final time, she'd leave a piece of her heart with him.

Eighteen

Ana called Zach's house, hoping to catch the housekeeper. Thankfully the Latina woman remembered her.

"I never see one of Mr. Marcum's ladies. I hear about them, but never see," she repeated with a heavy accent.

Okay, that was a plus in her favor, though Ana didn't really want to hear about all of Mr. Marcum's ladies. She asked the woman if she could stop by and pick up Jake for the day.

Now Ana was in a rental car, with towels placed all over the front seat and floor to help defer the mess of any accidental doggie business and she was heading to Zach's office for a surprise. Since he was always doing things for her, she decided to take half the day away from the site and spend it with him. After all, her mother would be in town tomorrow and Ana had barely mentioned the fact. What would he think of meeting her mother? Surely he knew, because she'd given her body so freely and confessed her feelings, that she wanted more from this relationship than just an occasional romp.

Ana found a parking spot directly in front of his office

s she exited the car, she squinted against the harsh gleam
f sunshine reflecting off the six-story glass office building.

A bubble of excitement popped up when she glanced in
he backseat at the large picnic basket and white blanket she'd
rought. She reached across the console and scooped up Jake,
ucking him under her arm.

When she stepped through the double doors, the re-
eptionist greeted her. "Good afternoon, Miss Clark. Are
ou here to see Mr. Marcum?"

Ana nodded. "But don't tell him I'm here. I want to surprise
im."

The young woman's eyes darted down the hall toward the
levator and back as she bit her lip. "Um…okay."

That was weird, Ana thought as she headed for the elevator.
Another woman, a very tall, stunning blonde, stood waiting
s well.

The doors slid open just as Ana got there.

"What a cute dog," the other woman said as they entered
he car together. "What's its name?"

Ana pushed the number four and said, "Jake. My boyfriend
ust bought him for me and I'm here to surprise him and take
im to lunch."

The elevator lifted and seconds later the doors opened on
he fourth floor.

"But I thought Cole just got married," the blonde said, her
rows drawn together.

Ana stepped off the elevator with the woman. "Oh, he did
ust Saturday. I'm dating his brother."

The woman's eyes widened, her mouth dropped open.
"Really? Well, I'm his wife."

Ana's hold on the dog tightened, but she was careful not
o squeeze too tight. No need in causing harm to the wrong
eing. Surely she heard wrong or this positively breathtaking
oman was delusional.

"You say Zach bought you the dog?" the beauty asked.

"Funny, he always told me he never wanted pets messing u our tidy house. But whatever. I didn't catch your name."

Ana refused to show any emotion and let this woman hav the upper hand, no matter that her heart had just taken punch. "If you'll excuse me," she muttered, purposely ignorin the request.

Just as she turned to go, the woman touched her arm. ' need to see him before you and Toto here go in."

From the corner of her eye Ana spotted Zach striding dow the hallway. And, oh, joy, the ex noticed at the same time, to They both watched an unknowing Zach as he came towar them with his head down, reading a document.

Ana ate up his looks from his shiny black shoes to hi faded designer jeans and long-sleeve black dress shirt rolle up onto his tanned forearms. Even his messy, spiky hair an stubble along the jawline didn't diminish the fact that th man was sexy. Sexy and very much in trouble.

"Zach."

Ana stood back, holding Jake to her chest as the ex crosse to him.

"Melanie." He jerked to a stop, then darted his eyes ov her shoulder to look straight at Ana. "Ana? What's goin on?"

Ana shrugged, letting Melanie have her say. No way w: she going to interrupt this. Seeing Zach's reaction to his would give her an insight into his true feelings—somethin she never doubted until now.

"I need to talk to you," Melanie said, throwing a glanc over her shoulder. "Alone."

Suddenly Ana wished she'd thrown on a cute sundres instead of her white shorts and blue tank. But she figure they'd be at the beach for the picnic and she wanted to b comfortable. Melanie, however, seemed to be comfortable i her skinny mini strapless dress and stilettos.

Yeah, Ana could so see Zach wanting to spend the rest

his life with an hourglass instead of a stick figure with a B cup…and that was on her "puffy" days.

Jake whimpered and Ana kissed his fur. "You're okay," she whispered in his little ear.

"After we talked the other day, I didn't hear from you so I thought I'd stop by and talk in person," Melanie said. "You didn't answer the texts I sent on Saturday night."

Saturday night. The night Ana had given herself to a man who was still in a relationship with his ex-wife. A viselike grip tightened around her heart and Ana couldn't hold back the gasp as air whooshed from her lungs.

Zach's eyes darted back to Ana, as if he knew where her thoughts had wandered. And if Melanie's revelation hadn't just ripped out her heart, the look in his dark eyes did.

Sorrow, shame, guilt, they all stared back at her. How long had they been talking? Is that why he'd been so patient with her? He was already getting some from his ex?

God, what a loser and gullible mess she was. But Ana refused to be the "other" woman as her mother had for years.

"If you'd just told me that you were in a serious relationship, I wouldn't be here," Melanie went on to say.

Zach looked back to Melanie and ran a hand through his hair. The other hand holding the document fell lazily to his side. "I didn't say anything because I'm not in a serious relationship."

"Really?" Melanie laughed. "Because this sure looks serious. A dog, Zach?"

If the fist around her heart hadn't been squeezing hard enough before, it sure was now. Ana refused to be the third party in whatever twisted relationship Zach and his ex obviously still had. She wanted out of here now, but she didn't want to look like she was jealous or hurt. No, she didn't want to give either of them the satisfaction of knowing how naive she'd been to believe a playboy like Zach Marcum could change.

"Go ahead and talk privately," Ana told them with a smile she knew looked just as fake as it felt. "I need to take Jake outside anyway."

She turned to go and Zach called out her name. Ignoring him, she punched the elevator button.

"Ana." He grabbed her arm. "I'm sorry."

"What? Sorry you lied or sorry that you got caught?" Venom all but dripped from each word. "Don't apologize when you don't mean it."

"I do. Don't leave like this. Let me explain."

Glaring over her shoulder at him, she jerked her arm free and brought both hands up to Jake who was now trying to get to Zach. "Don't worry. You told me when you told your *wife* exactly what we have. We're not serious, so go talk with Melanie and any other woman you desire. Just make sure it's not me."

The doors slid open and Ana stepped onto the elevator. As she turned, the doors closed, shutting her off from Zach's angry face and Melanie's triumphant glare.

Ana couldn't get to her car fast enough. She ran by the receptionist who Ana noticed gave her a quick, apologetic smile.

Finally alone, Ana sat Jake in the passenger seat and squealed the tires as she pulled away from the curb. She didn't want to be in the vicinity of Zach Marcum for a long time. She actually never wanted to see him again, but since they weren't done with the resort yet, that would be impossible.

Wonderful. Just wonderful. She would have to see him every day for the next several months. Thankfully the exterior was near completion and her men would be mostly working inside now. There would be plenty of room for her to hide in the monstrous resort when Zach came to check on things. She'd just have her second-in-command fill Mr. Marcum in on the progress.

Ana turned down another palm-lined road. She really had no clue where she was going; she just needed to drive.

All of this was her own fault. Every bit of it. So why was she mad at Zach? He'd told her up front that he didn't do relationships. Hadn't he said marriage had sucked the love right out of him? He hadn't lied to her about that. But he had lied, at least by omission.

That was the part that hurt the most. He had been talking with his ex the whole time he'd been trying to get her into bed. He'd been so convincing that he cared about her feelings, so gentle when they'd finally made love.

Made love. Yeah. That was totally one-sided. No wonder he panicked when she professed her love to him. What a total idiot, she thought, hating herself more and more with each passing moment.

Ana pulled her car off the road and parked facing the beach. With her head in her hands, she let the tears fall, one right after the other, angry at herself for letting anyone in that could cause this much damage to her heart again.

Why hadn't she seen the signs? Why? Even after she'd opened up and told him how she felt about him, that she loved him, he still hadn't confessed. His silence spoke volumes; too bad she was just now hearing it.

Jake crossed the console and slid his sandpaper-like puppy tongue along the tears that seeped through her fingers.

Yes, all of this mess was her fault and that made her a complete idiot. But the fact that she still loved him made her a damn fool.

"Oh, honey. Now don't do this to yourself."

Ana sat on her bed, sobbing into her mother's loving arms. "I can't help it. I've tried to hate him. I've even tried to push his betrayal out of my mind, but that's all I can think of."

Lorraine Clark stroked her daughter's hair and leaned back against the satin-covered headboard. "Has he tried to call?"

Ana slid her head down into her mother's lap and let the gentle stroking of her long hair relax her as much as it could. "He's tried. I won't answer. I'm such a coward. I even called out of work today. But since it's Friday, that wasn't a big deal. My crew can handle one day. Besides, I'm hoping by Monday I'll be better."

"Why can't you go to the site?" her mother asked.

Ana closed her eyes and wiped her damp cheeks. "Because he's the architect for the project. He's at the site at least once a day."

"Oh, Anastasia."

Her mother's soft tone and simple words only made Ana ache more. Even her mother noticed the severity of the situation. Of course her mother would notice. Her mother had lived through a lifetime of pure hell.

But now she was free. They both were—thanks to Zach.

Another heart-wrenching sob tore through her. Not even her mother's soothing words and comforting presence could help repair her shattered world.

She had to get this out now. No way would she show even an inkling of sadness on the site.

"I hate being weak," she murmured into her mother's long crinkle skirt. "I hate knowing that I let someone get that close to me when I knew the outcome. I knew this would happen, but I didn't care. Deep down I thought I would be the one. Foolish, really, to think the one time I find myself attracted enough for a relationship, it's with someone like him."

Her mother's hands stilled in her hair. "You love him."

"I don't want to."

Lorraine let out a soft sigh. "Unfortunately we don't choose whom we love. Right or wrong, sometimes our hearts and our heads don't communicate well."

Ana sat up, wiped her eyes again and sniffed. "I'm sorry

to have a meltdown the second you get here. You're dealing with your own problems."

Her mother smiled and reached for Ana's hands. "No matter what's going on in my life, I'm never too busy for you."

Ana studied her mother's creamy skin, the slight wrinkles around her eyes and mouth. With blond, shoulder-length hair and bright green eyes, Lorraine Clark was a beauty even at the age of sixty. The woman didn't look much over forty and Ana knew how lucky she was to have at least one parent who would drop anything to be with the ones she loved.

"What is wrong with Dad?" Ana asked before she could stop herself. "I'm sorry. That was rude."

"That's okay. I've often wondered what I could have done differently." A sad smile formed as Lorraine looked across the room out the window toward the bay. "It took me a long time to realize it wasn't me at all. He wasn't the man I wanted him to be. We didn't have the relationship I conjured up in my head."

"Why did you stay?"

Her mother's gaze came back to Ana. "Fear of being alone. I'd been with him so long that I didn't know if I could make it on my own. Plus when you were younger, I was so worried I wouldn't be able to take care of you financially. Of course, I had no idea he'd started gambling away everything we had."

Ana embraced her mother. "Let's do something for ourselves today. What do you say we take advantage of the spa in this hotel? We need to be pampered."

Lorraine eased back and smiled. "I couldn't agree more. And no more talk about love and foolishness. This is girls' day."

Ana could go the rest of the day and not discuss Zach, but that didn't mean he wouldn't always be in the forefront of her mind. The only way she could get over him was to move on.

From here on out all she would concentrate on would be work and her mother.

What else did she need?

Nineteen

Zach pulled his Screamin' Eagle onto the site.

Two weeks had passed since he'd talked, alone, to Ana. Every time he came to the site, she was inside the resort and her assistant foreman had filled him in on where the project stood. One time she wasn't around because she'd gone to run an errand—one that he could've done had she called him and admitted she needed help.

She refused to return his calls, ignored his texts. God, she was acting like…him. Zach killed the roaring engine and stared at the beautiful gigantic resort. Ana was brushing him off like he'd done to women when they got too close. Only when Ana had gotten close, he wasn't nearly as ready to get rid of her as he had been every woman in the past.

But now she acted as if nothing had happened between them, as if they hadn't changed each other's lives. And, yes, she had changed his life. He couldn't pinpoint when, but she had.

Anger flooded through him. Hadn't she told him she loved

him? That was something she couldn't just turn off. Unless she hadn't meant it to begin with. But Zach knew Ana never said anything if she didn't mean it. Could he have killed that love so quickly? He didn't want to even consider the notion.

Zach wanted to make Ana listen. Make her understand that Melanie wasn't part of his life anymore. He was over her.

Had been over her.

It just took seeing the two women side by side to come to grips with what he already knew.

Ana had been standing there in her little shorts and tank with her wild red curls, holding their dog, and Melanie had looked like the knockout she was with every hair in place, every nail professionally polished to a shine. But it had been Ana to whom his body had responded.

Zach stopped dead in his tracks on the dusty path to Ana's office. He'd called Jake "their" dog. Since when was Jake "their" dog?

Making his feet move again, Zach realized that the dog had been theirs from the get-go. Obviously even then he knew he cared for her more than he wanted, more than he thought possible.

Behind his dark shades, he scanned the area. Ana wasn't in sight, so he made his way toward her office. He tapped lightly on the door, but didn't wait for her to respond or answer. He walked right in—and froze.

Ana sat at her desk, and a woman probably around forty or so sat opposite her. The two were sharing lunch and laughing, but their faces froze and all chatter ceased when he entered.

"I didn't mean to interrupt," he said, closing the door behind him. "Ana, I need to speak with you."

Ana set down her fork in her salad and came to her feet. "I'm having lunch with my mother, Zach. Is this about business?"

Zach's eyes darted back to the other woman. Good Lord,

that woman was Ana's *mother?* She was stunning, poised; obviously she'd aged very well.

"I'm Zach Marcum." He extended his hand. "I see where Ana gets her beauty from."

The woman came to her feet, smiled and shook his hand. "She said you were charming. I'm Lorraine Clark."

Zach held on to her hand, quirked a brow over at Ana. "She's mentioned me, huh?"

"Only as a warning," Ana said, unsmiling. "What do you need?"

He dropped Lorraine's hand and shoved his hands in his denim pockets. "The same thing I've needed for weeks. To talk to you alone."

Ana mimicked his stance by placing her hands on her hips. "Surely you of all people recognize a brush-off, Zach. Isn't that how you work? Go back to Melanie or whoever else you want this week. I'm not interested."

If she didn't care that her mother overheard their conversation, then neither did he. "I'm not interested in Melanie. I want you."

Ana stared, then looked down at her desk, but he didn't miss the moisture that gathered in her eyes or the way she blinked rapidly trying to keep her emotions hidden.

"Well, we can't always have what we want." Ana's tone softened, and her throat sounded full of tears and emotions. She picked up her salad and tossed it into the garbage. "Now, if that's all, I'd like to finish talking with my mother."

Zach nodded, refusing to grovel for anything. He'd caused this damage and now he had to live with it.

"It was a pleasure to meet you." He offered Lorraine a smile even though he wanted to yell or throw something, anything to make Ana listen. "I need to speak to the assistant foreman before I leave. If you'll excuse me."

He left the office without looking back. If she was truly

done, then he would walk away and leave her be. But he didn't believe she was because she couldn't look him in the eye.

Zach did a one-eighty and got back on his bike. He didn't need to speak to the foreman that badly. There was something much more important he had to do. A plan formed in his mind and he knew this could seriously make or break his future.

For once in his life, he was putting business on the back burner, putting himself second and putting a woman first.

He didn't know another term for this insane way of thinking. It must be love.

Ana was so looking forward to a weekend with no contact with Zach. She and her mother had planned a glorious day at the beach doing nothing but soaking up the sun and catching up on some reading…something Ana hadn't done in, well, she couldn't remember how long.

While her mother changed in the bedroom of the suite, Ana threw some bottles of water, a book and a towel into her yellow mesh bag. The day at the spa they'd had together last weekend was great, but Ana needed another day of relaxation. Especially after Zach had confronted her in front of her mother.

God, she wished he'd just see what she was offering. Why couldn't he see how fake Melanie was? Ana had been in the other woman's presence for all of five minutes and was less than impressed.

If that's what Zach found attractive, then obviously she was the wrong woman for him. But oh, how she wished he weren't that shallow. She truly believed he wasn't, but he was rich and perhaps he'd gotten swept into that lifestyle. Ana had been in Miami long enough to realize that image was everything.

The ache that had taken up permanent residence in her heart grew deeper roots each day. The way Zach had listened to her, had offered advice when it came to her father and her childhood, the way he knew what would make her smile and laugh all were indications he cared for, if not loved, her.

He'd bought her a dog, for crying out loud. Hadn't his ex even said he'd forbidden a dog in their house?

She replayed every moment they'd spent together, over and over, and she never saw a spot where he acted like he didn't want to be with her.

Each flash of memory was filled with laughter and unspoken promises.

Maybe she'd just gotten wrapped up in Zach because she'd given herself to him, but Ana highly doubted it.

Dammit, she just wanted to find a reason or a person to place blame on. But she knew blame could only lie with herself. She knew going in what kind of man Zach was.

"All ready."

Her mother's cheery tone snapped Ana out of her stroll down agony lane.

Lorraine stepped from the bedroom wearing her one-piece red bathing suit with a black wrap around her hips. "Let me just grab my bag."

A heavy knock sounded on the door. "Okay, I'll get the door," Ana called over her shoulder.

Ana moved through the living area and opened the door. To Zach. Holding Jake.

"He missed you," Zach said, holding the dog out.

Taking Jake, Ana held him against her chest and swallowed that lump of emotion that came along with seeing Zach. "Thanks. Mom and I are going out. I'll take him with us."

Zach shoved his hands in his pockets and leaned against the doorjamb. "I was hoping you'd come with me. I have something to show you."

Ana didn't want to be standing this close to him, let alone go anywhere with him. The spicy, clean aroma she'd grown accustomed to from Zach wafted around her. The sexy stubble he always seemed to have was just a tad longer than usual.

His eyes were puffy as if he hadn't slept and his hair was downright unkempt. Ana knew those long, tanned fingers had run through that thick hair over and over.

As much as she enjoyed that he was looking as miserable as she felt, she still loved the man, even though she wanted to throttle him for taking her heart and crushing it with both hands.

"That's not a good idea, Zach."

"I think it's a great idea," her mother said, stepping up behind her. "Go on, Ana. We can go to the beach next weekend when you're off."

Ana turned to her mother. "What will you do?"

Lorraine smiled. "Don't worry about me. I'll just take a book and pick out a nice lounge chair with an umbrella and relax. Now go on."

Even though Ana hated to admit it, she was curious as to what he wanted to show her. And to be honest, she knew they needed to talk. They couldn't leave things up in the air even though Ana knew the outcome. Stepping out that door with Zach would just bring on more heartache, but after all she'd given him she deserved the chance to speak and let him know where she stood.

"All right." Ana turned back to Zach. "Let me grab my bag."

"You won't need anything," he told her. "Just Jake."

Hesitant, Ana decided to leave her belongings, except her key, which she slid into her shorts pocket. She kissed her mother goodbye, made sure she had the spare key and followed Zach out the door.

Silence surrounded them in the hallway, accompanied them into the elevator and settled between them once they were in his truck.

Okay, so obviously he wasn't in a talkative mood. She

could deal with that…for now. Eventually they would have to talk, but she would go with his flow until they got to the surprise destination.

When they pulled into his driveway, he hopped out and came around to help her down from the truck. She kept hold of Jake as she followed him into his house.

"Come into my office."

Ana set Jake down and went with Zach. The little puppy's paws clicked on the marble floor behind her as she entered Zach's spacious office. Ana couldn't help but admire the beauty of the floor-to-ceiling windows on the two exterior walls. His lavish, well-manicured gardens were quite the view and definitely could inspire anyone working at the oversize mahogany desk.

And it was the desk that drew her attention now. Sprawled across it were blueprints.

"Before you look at this, I need you to know something."

Ana risked taking her gaze from the harmless paper up to Zach's dark eyes. "What?"

"Your father won't be a problem for you anymore. I paid off all his debts and he signed a legal, binding document not to come in contact with you or your mother ever again. Not in person, not via the internet or phone or any other form of communication."

Ana sucked in a breath. "Why did you do that?"

The muscle in Zach's jaw ticked as he glanced down to the desk. "I want no secrets between us."

With a mock laugh, Ana crossed her arms. "Too late for that, isn't it?"

"Look over these," he told her with a roughness to his tone as he pointed down to the drawings. "I'm looking for a company to build this."

Ana swallowed hard. "Zach, after this resort is done, my company is moving on. We have a six-story office building to construct in Dallas. Besides, I don't think it's a good idea for us to work together anymore. Let's just finish these last two months and put this behind us."

"Can you just look at the plans?" he pleaded.

Stepping up to the desk, Ana looked down, but it didn't take her long to see this wasn't any commercial project. "This is a house. I don't generally contract homes." She studied the amazing plans, though, nearly salivating at the lucky would-be owner. "Who wants this done? Victor?"

"Me."

Ana looked up. "You?"

Oh, God. Just drive the knife in and give it a swift turn, why don't ya? Now he expected her to build a home where he could resume residence with his ex-wife. Yeah, she should've listened to her first instincts and not gone with him today. She should be sitting on the beach with a fruity little drink, reading the latest gossip magazines with her mother.

Instead she and her heart were here, taking another beating. Was Melanie somewhere in the house? Did she still have that smirk Ana so wanted to smack off?

Ana glanced to the door, half expecting the ex to be keeping watch over Zach. "Does Melanie know you're asking me to build her house?"

Zach came around his desk and stood within inches of her. Ana tipped her head back to look into his heavy-lidded dark eyes.

"You're not building a house for Melanie. You'd be building a house for me…and you."

Hope, hurt, stress in general all plagued her at once and Ana couldn't look him in the eyes another second. She turned, crossed the room to sit on the bulky leather couch. As much as she wanted to believe, she couldn't look at him, couldn't let herself get drawn back into the dark depth of his eyes, his world.

She curled her feet beneath her, rubbed her damp palms down the cover-up she'd thrown over her swimsuit. "Don't. Just don't. This can't happen, Zach."

"What can't happen?"

Ana shoved her stray curls from her face and lifted her gaze to his. "Whatever you have planned. You aren't over your ex, that's obvious. And that's okay. I knew you weren't long-term when I got involved with you. Part of this mess is my fault, but please don't make me believe in something you can't give."

Zach closed the gap between them, crouched down to take her hands in his. "You're right. When we first met I wasn't in a place where I could, or even wanted to, get involved with someone. I was hung up on Melanie even if I didn't admit it to myself."

Hearing those words, knowing he meant them didn't help the tight band around her chest. If anything, he'd just pulled it tighter.

"But you changed everything," he admitted. "I never wanted another relationship, but I can't deny myself. I can't walk away from you."

Ana stared into his eyes, saw the shimmer of his own unshed tears. "How can I believe you? How do I know you don't just want me because you lost me? What if you decided next month you're ready to move on? You've even admitted yourself that you're always looking for something better."

He nodded and tucked a curl behind her ear before squeezing her hands. "I was, but I found something better. You. You're the something I'd always been looking for."

That hope that had started forming in her heart when she'd seen the house plans grew just a bit more. "What about Melanie? You love her."

"No, I don't." He eased up next to her on the couch and

faced her fully. "I thought I loved her, and maybe I did on some level, but whatever I felt for her is absolutely nothing compared to the feelings I have for you."

Ana leaned in closer to Zach. She wanted to look in his eyes when she asked the next question. Wanted to look for any doubt, and lie.

"What do you feel for me?"

"Love." A wide smile lit his face. "I admit, when I first realized I loved you, I denied it to myself. I didn't want to get hurt again."

Ana didn't even try to stop the tears from falling now. "Hurt? You destroyed me when I found out you'd been talking with Melanie. To know that you love me... God, Zach, that's more than I ever thought you'd feel for me. I want to believe..."

Zach cupped her damp cheeks in his palms, pulled her against him for a hard, loving kiss. Yes, loving. She felt it in every part of her. He did love her.

Ana wrapped her arms around his neck, unable to control her emotions a moment longer.

"Believe," he murmured against her lips. His forehead rested against hers. "Ana, believe in everything I'm telling you. Don't doubt my love for you. Ever."

Ana couldn't speak for the tears, so she nodded.

"Is that a yes that you'll build our house?" he asked.

"Y-yes." She sniffled. "I knew you loved me, Zach. I just never knew if you'd see it yourself. Months ago when I poured my heart out to you about my childhood you listened. You've been so patient, so understanding. I know what I've found in you will make me happier than I deserve to be for the rest of my life."

He eased back, wiping her tears with the pads of his thumbs. "I have another condition."

"What?"

"We only have a couple months left on Victor's resort, then you can send your crew on to Dallas, but I want you here for a while."

Ana drew her brows together. "I'll have to go get things started, Zach. I can't just forget this project because you asked me to. What is so important?"

"Marry me," he said with a smile. "Tell me you'll stay in my life forever."

Stunned, elated, nervous. Ana didn't know what label to place on all the feelings whirling around in her mind, her heart.

"Are you sure?" she asked, praying to God he was. "You married before and swore you'd never marry again."

"That's because I married the wrong woman. Everything about you, about us, is right."

Ana grabbed hold of Zach's strong hands as he continued to hold her face. "I want babies and more dogs."

Zach kissed her again, his mouth hard, possessive. He wrapped his arms around her waist, pulled her tight against him.

"More of anything with you is fine with me," he told her as he eased her back against the couch, already working her sheer cover-up off. "I have another surprise for you."

"I've seen it." She laughed.

"Oh, well, I do have that," he joked. "But I bought you your own bike. It's in my garage."

She held a hand to his chest to stop him. "My own motorcycle?"

"Well, yeah. I want you riding with me."

Ana ran the possibility through her mind and nodded. "I suppose since you were my first with everything, you may as well teach me to ride. Provided we can get to actually start the engine this time."

Zach's smile remained in place, but his eyes grew serious as he explored her face. "You were my first, too. Love never meant anything to me until you, Anastasia Clark."

Ana knew this journey she was about to embark on with Zach was just the start of many firsts to come.

* * * * *

COMING NEXT MONTH

Available May 10, 2011

#2083 KING'S MILLION-DOLLAR SECRET
Maureen Child
Kings of California

#2084 EXPOSED: HER UNDERCOVER MILLIONAIRE
Michelle Celmer
The Takeover

#2085 SECRET SON, CONVENIENT WIFE
Maxine Sullivan
Billionaires and Babies

#2086 TEXAS-SIZED TEMPTATION
Sara Orwig
Stetsons & CEOs

#2087 DANTE'S HONOR-BOUND HUSBAND
Day Leclaire
The Dante Legacy

#2088 CARRYING THE RANCHER'S HEIR
Charlene Sands

You can find more information on upcoming
Harlequin® titles, free excerpts and more at
www.HarlequinInsideRomance.com.

REQUEST YOUR FREE BOOKS!
2 FREE NOVELS PLUS 2 FREE GIFTS!

Harlequin

Desire

ALWAYS POWERFUL, PASSIONATE AND PROVOCATIVE

YES! Please send me 2 FREE Harlequin Desire® novels and my 2 FREE gifts (gifts are worth about $10). After receiving them, if I don't wish to receive any more books, I can return the shipping statement marked "cancel." If I don't cancel, I will receive 6 brand-new novels every month and be billed just $4.05 per book in the U.S. or $4.74 per book in Canada. That's a saving of at least 15% off the cover price! It's quite a bargain! Shipping and handling is just 50¢ per book in the U.S. and 75¢ per book in Canada.* I understand that accepting the 2 free books and gifts places me under no obligation to buy anything. I can always return a shipment and cancel at any time. Even if I never buy another book, the two free books and gifts are mine to keep forever.

225/326 SDN FC65

Name _____ (PLEASE PRINT) _____

Address _____ Apt. #

City _____ State/Prov. _____ Zip/Postal Code

Signature (if under 18, a parent or guardian must sign)

Mail to the **Reader Service:**

IN U.S.A.: P.O. Box 1867, Buffalo, NY 14240-1867
IN CANADA: P.O. Box 609, Fort Erie, Ontario L2A 5X3

Not valid for current subscribers to Harlequin Desire books.

Want to try two free books from another line?
Call 1-800-873-8635 or visit www.ReaderService.com.

* Terms and prices subject to change without notice. Prices do not include applicable taxes. Sales tax applicable in N.Y. Canadian residents will be charged applicable taxes. Offer not valid in Quebec. This offer is limited to one order per household. All orders subject to credit approval. Credit or debit balances in a customer's account(s) may be offset by any other outstanding balance owed by or to the customer. Please allow 4 to 6 weeks for delivery. Offer available while quantities last.

Your Privacy—The Reader Service is committed to protecting your privacy. Our Privacy Policy is available online at www.ReaderService.com or upon request from the Reader Service.

We make a portion of our mailing list available to reputable third parties that offer products we believe may interest you. If you prefer that we not exchange your name with third parties, or if you wish to clarify or modify your communication preferences, please visit us at www.ReaderService.com/consumerchoice or write to us at Reader Service Preference Service, P.O. Box 9062, Buffalo, NY 14269. Include your complete name and address.

HDES11

With an evil force hell-bent on destruction, two enemies must unite to find a truth that turns all-too-personal when passions collide.

Enjoy a sneak peek in Jenna Kernan's next installment in her original TRACKER *series, GHOST STALKER, available in May, only from Harlequin Nocturne.*

"**W**ho are you?" he snarled.

Jessie lifted her chin. "Your better."

His smile was cold. "Such arrogance could only come from a Niyanoka."

She nodded. "Why are you here?"

"I don't know." He glanced about her room. "I asked the birds to take me to a healer."

"And they have done so. Is that *all* you asked?"

"No. To lead them away from my friends." His eyes fluttered and she saw them roll over white.

Jessie straightened, preparing to flee, but he roused himself and mastered the momentary weakness. His eyes snapped open, locking on her.

Her heart hammered as she inched back.

"Lead who away?" she whispered, suddenly afraid of the answer.

"The ghosts. Nagi sent them to attack me so I would bring them to her."

The wolf must be deranged because Nagi did not send ghosts to attack living creatures. He captured the evil ones after their death if they refused to walk the Way of Souls, forcing them to face judgment.

"Her? The healer you seek is also female?"

"Michaela. She's Niyanoka, like you. The last Seer of Souls and Nagi wants her dead."

Jessie fell back to her seat on the carpet as the possibility of this ricocheted in her brain. Could it be true?

"Why should I believe you?" But she knew why. His black aura, the part that said he had been touched by death. Only a ghost could do that. But it made no sense.

Why would Nagi hunt one of her people and why would a Skinwalker want to protect her? She had been trained from birth to hate the Skinwalkers, to consider them a threat.

His intent blue eyes pinned her. Jessie felt her mouth go dry as she considered the impossible. Could the trickster be speaking the truth? Great Mystery, what evil was this?

She stared in astonishment. There was only one way to find her answers. But she had never even met a Skinwalker before and so did not even know if they dreamed.

But if he dreamed, she would have her chance to learn the truth.

*Look for GHOST STALKER by Jenna Kernan,
available May only from Harlequin Nocturne,
wherever books and ebooks are sold.*

Harlequin® *Desire*

ALWAYS POWERFUL, PASSIONATE AND PROVOCATIVE.

USA TODAY BESTSELLING AUTHOR

MAUREEN CHILD

BRINGS YOU ANOTHER PASSIONATE TALE

KINGS *of* CALIFORNIA

KING'S MILLION-DOLLAR SECRET

Rafe King was labeled as the King who didn't know how to love. And even he believed it. That is, until the day he met Katie Charles. The one woman who shows him taking chances in life can reap the best rewards. Even when the odds are stacked against you.

Available May, wherever books are sold.

American ★ Romance®

Fan favorite author
TINA LEONARD
is back with
an exciting new miniseries.

Six bachelor brothers are given a challenge—
get married, start a big family and whoever does
so first will inherit the famed Rancho Diablo.
Too bad none of these cowboys is marriage material!

Callahan Cowboys:
Catch one if you can!

The Cowboy's Triplets (May 2011)
The Cowboy's Bonus Baby (July 2011)
The Bull Rider's Twins (Sept 2011)
Bonus Callahan Christmas Novella! (Nov 2011)
His Valentine Triplets (Jan 2012)
Cowboy Sam's Quadruplets (March 2012)
A Callahan Wedding (May 2012)